P9-DNB-501

HELEN FOX

WENDY
LAMB
BOOKS

eager's
nephew

Published by Wendy Lamb Books
an imprint of Random House Children's Books
a division of Random House, Inc.
New York

WENDY LAMB BOOKS and colophon are trademarks of Random House, Inc.

www.randomhouse.com/kids

Educators and librarians, for a variety of teaching tools,
visit us at www.randomhouse.com/teachers

Library of Congress Cataloging-in-Publication Data

Fox, Helen.
Eager's nephew / Helen Fox.
p. cm.
Summary: In a world which has banned self-aware robots, Eager and his brilliant but headstrong nephew, Jonquil, come out of hiding to visit the Bell family, and soon become involved in the mysterious and dangerous events surrounding them and their friends.
ISBN-13: 978-0-385-74673-1 (hardcover)—ISBN-13: 978-0-385-90904-4 (lib. bdg.)
ISBN-10: 0-385-74673-3 (hardcover)—ISBN-10: 0-385-90904-7 (lib. bdg.)
[1. Robots—Fiction. 2. Science fiction.] I. Title.
PZ7.F833Eah 2006
[Fic]—dc22
2006004297

Printed in the United States of America

10 9 8 7 6 5 4 3 2 1

First Edition

For my parents and stepparents,

with love

PROLOGUE

Professor Ogden sat at a gobetween, checking a calculation. It was his custom to work late, long after his colleagues had gone home. He paid no attention to the sound of footsteps behind him: an animat, no doubt, come to clean the laboratory.

"Good evening, Professor," said a familiar voice.

"Mr. Lobsang!" The professor sprang from his chair. He shook his former colleague's hand. "I thought you were in Tibet, enjoying your retirement."

The Tibetan wore wire-rimmed glasses. It was hard to see his expression in the low light. "I had business here, but I return later tonight," he said. He clapped his hands together in a theatrical manner. "What about a drink before I leave, Bill?"

Professor Ogden tried not to smile. In all his years at LifeCorp, Mr. Lobsang had never been seen in the company bar. It was doubtful that he even knew where it was.

"Or would you prefer a walk in the grounds?"

"I would welcome some fresh air," said the professor. He noticed that his visitor looked relieved.

It was dusk. LifeCorp's vast headquarters loomed behind them as they strolled through the landscaped garden. Mr. Lobsang described how he was spending his days in Tibet. When they were some distance from the main building, his tone changed.

"The battle is lost," he said gravely. "A law will be passed next month forbidding anyone to create self-aware robots."

Professor Ogden looked at him quizzically. "Self-aware?"

"The law defines it as 'robots that can reflect on their actions and feel emotion.'"

"Ah," said the professor.

The Tibetan gave a short laugh. "Of course, we all know such robots do not exist. Nobody knows how to make one. But from now on, researching, teaching or even discussing the subject in public is banned. The punishment will be prison."

Professor Ogden fixed his gaze on a distant flower bed. "What would happen to the robot?" he asked. "Were a scientist ever to build one that was self-aware?"

"It would be destroyed."

They walked on in silence.

Mr. Lobsang said in a low voice, "Ten years ago, Bill, your robot, Eager, saved my life. He did it of his own free will, I am sure of that. But I do not believe that he is self-aware. Nonetheless, I made a vow to protect him. All these years, I have fought to

2

stop the law being introduced. There is a lot of fear, as you know, that conscious robots will be a danger to humans."

Professor Ogden said abruptly, "But why now? After all this time?"

"There are rumors that some countries are building intelligent robots as war machines. It is hoped that this new law will stop them."

Professor Ogden shook his head. "When will we ever learn?"

A surveillance pod appeared from behind a large bush. It hovered in front of them for a moment. Mr. Lobsang began talking about the view from the window of his study. "Snow-covered mountains," he said. "I can see for miles. . . ."

The pod whirred and flew in the opposite direction.

Mr. Lobsang laid a hand on the professor's arm. "Listen, I am here to warn you. When this law comes into force your robot will be in danger. He is still with the Bell family, I take it?"

Professor Ogden nodded. "He's due to return and help me with my work. The older children have grown up and left home, but the youngest, Charlotte, is not yet twelve. He's been with her since she was a baby, so we decided to wait a couple more years. . . ." He sighed. "I suppose he will have to join me sooner."

"Are you mad?" Mr. Lobsang shook Professor Ogden's arm.

The professor looked at him in surprise.

"You must understand, Bill. Every government in the world is signing the new law. Nowhere is safe anymore. And where is the first place they will look for him?"

"With me . . . ," said Professor Ogden. He sounded stunned. "But I can't leave him with the Bells."

"You are too attached to him to think clearly. Whatever you do, act quickly," said Mr. Lobsang.

They came to the outer wall of the grounds and turned to walk back.

"This new law—they call it the Ban," continued Mr. Lobsang. "You realize that you will be expected to sign it?"

Professor Ogden focused his attention on the gravel path. "Did LifeCorp ask you to speak to me?"

Mr. Lobsang did not reply directly. "Naturally they are interested in your response. But you can trust me. Your secret is safe." He paused. "Well? What is your answer? Will you sign?"

"Tell them I shall refuse," said Professor Ogden.

Mr. Lobsang sighed. "I expected as much. They will ask you to resign, of course."

"Of course," said the professor softly.

The two men shook hands outside the main entrance.

"Good luck," said Mr. Lobsang. He added under his breath, "To both of you."

TEN YEARS LATER

CHAPTER 1.

Eager looked out of the flying pod at the familiar streets. Soon he would be at the Bells' house. He remembered the first time he had made the journey. He had said goodbye to Professor Ogden, his creator, to go and live with the Bell family. "I was only a few weeks old and everything was new to me," thought Eager. "I couldn't even put a name to my feelings. Now I know that I was feeling sad at leaving the professor, but I was also excited and curious to be out in the world at last."

He lived with the Bells for many years, until it became unsafe to stay among humans. Professor Ogden found him a hiding place, but although Eager learned to live in isolation he missed the family badly. Ten years had passed, and each summer he ventured from the secret address to pay a short visit to the Bells.

Now Eager was feeling a strange mix of emotions once again. The thought of being with the Bells gave him great pleasure. But the long months of separation that would follow made him feel sad.

He imagined what he might do during his stay. Mr. Bell, who

had become a well-known architect, would tell him about his latest projects and show them to him on the gobetween. He might even take him to visit a building in progress.

Mrs. Bell worked part-time for LifeCorp, the company that built the animats. Professor Ogden had encouraged her to take the job, even though he had retired as head of robotics. "These animats may look like us, but they're really no more intelligent than my toaster," he said. "At least with your help we can program them to work sensibly." So Mrs. Bell produced job descriptions to help the designers program the robots. The rest of the week she was at home.

Eager looked forward to many friendly chats as he helped her in the kitchen.

And he would see Charlotte and Gavin and Fleur. The Bells' three children were adults now and lived away, but Eager knew that they would almost certainly come and see him during the week.

The moment he saw the turning to Wynston Avenue he told the delivery pod to stop. It was night and there was no one around, but Eager climbed out of the pod as quickly as he could.

"The distance traveled has been charged to your account," said the pod. "Thank you for your custom."

"Continue," Eager said in a low voice.

He waited for the pod to fly away before turning the corner into the avenue. It was so late that most of the houses had turned off their lights and closed the blinds. All the same, Eager paused outside each one to see if he could spot any changes, until excitement outweighed his curiosity. He extended the rubber rings of his legs and strode on.

As Eager stepped beyond the glare of a streetlamp, an object shot past his shoulder. "Sphere!" he whispered, expecting to see the luminous ball that sometimes appeared to guide him. It was not unlike Sphere to turn up out of the blue with a message, or simply to encourage him on his way.

But this object did not give off light or hover in the air as Sphere would have done. Instead, it landed on the ground ahead of Eager with a dry crackle, like the sound of twigs being dropped.

Eager had heard that noise many times. Peering into the darkness, he said in disbelief, "Jonquil?"

The object rolled forward into the pool of light from the next streetlamp. Eager saw that it was a hollow ball, its outer shell a loose weave of gossamer-fine fibers.

The ball unfurled itself. The fibers reassembled as a flat surface, like a stringy sheet of paper. The sheet stood upright, balancing itself on one edge. Since it had no features and no identifiable head or body, it was impossible to tell how it could speak. It spoke, nonetheless, in a thin treble, too quiet to be detected by anyone but Eager.

"Yes, it's me, Uncle Eager! You jumped out of that pod so fast, I was nearly left behind!"

Eager was dumbfounded. To think that he had journeyed two hours in the delivery pod, and Jonquil had been with him all along! "What were you doing in the pod?"

"I was being a passenger, like you," said Jonquil.

Eager looked over his shoulder toward the main road. It was not too late to find another pod and send his wayward nephew home. . . .

"You mustn't send me back," said Jonquil, understanding the glance.

"I wish you could stay, Jonquil," said Eager. "But it isn't safe for you here. Besides, you are not ready. Living in the human world takes practice."

"Only when you have to do things the human way," said Jonquil, tilting himself so that he stood on one corner. "You're designed to move like a human, with arms and legs and eyes, and to think like one too. But I'm not. I can do things my way. If I'd been trapped in that delivery pod just now I would have got out somehow, you know I would."

Eager nodded. He imagined his nephew roaming freely in the human world. He would certainly do things his way. If a door didn't open for him, he'd slide underneath it. If a cat chased him, he'd fly away. If a machine didn't do what he wanted, he could enter the controls and reprogram it. . . . These images made Eager even more anxious.

"You must go back," he said firmly.

He noticed that Jonquil had not moved for several seconds. The sheet balanced on one corner still, as if rooted to the spot.

"Are you all right?" he asked.

"Uncle Eager, it's so noisy!"

Eager's hearing was more acute than a human's; Jonquil's was many times more sensitive. As Eager tried to listen through Jonquil's ears, he was overwhelmed by the din. The trees, rustling gently, shrieked at him. Distant traffic howled in the darkness, while a few meters away, padding feet thundered down a garden path.

"Grrrrrr . . ."

To Jonquil, the growl was an explosion. He leapt into the air and flattened himself against Eager's chest. "What is that?" he said, so faintly that even Eager did not hear him.

"It won't harm us, it's behind the gate," said Eager. He added, "It was a dog. Now do you understand? Life here is threatening."

"I'm not scared of a dog," said Jonquil. "I can move faster than it can." He became round again and dropped to the pavement, where he began to roll, gathering speed. Abruptly he sprang into the air, thrusting out his fibers and shaking himself like a mop head. "The ground attacked me!" he cried.

Eager looked down. There was nothing on the pavement that he could see. "Dust," he said. "You must have brushed it into the air." Jonquil was sensitive to fine particles. "Be careful. There's dirt everywhere. You can't protect yourself in this world if you don't know the dangers."

Jonquil flew into the air and settled on Eager's shoulder. "I'm ready for anything! I've survived a dog and dust already."

Eager walked on with Jonquil perched on his shoulder. He saw the familiar bend in the road ahead of them, and the shape of the Bells' lime tree.

"Jonquil, you must go home. When I get to the Bells' house, I'll call a pod to take you back."

"Please, Uncle Eager, I've come all this way to be with you."

"It's too dangerous. You don't know enough."

"How will I know anything unless I go out into the world? How will I ever find out who I am?"

"You're a robot like me," said Eager. He corrected himself: "In some ways like me."

"But what does it mean to be a robot?" said Jonquil. "And what kind of a robot am I?"

Eager tilted his head to increase the thinking power to his brain. Twenty years ago, he'd been like Jonquil. Had he not been called Eager because of his enthusiasm, his urge to learn? Professor Ogden had sent him into the world to discover things for himself. Jonquil was right: in order to learn, he would have to step into the unknown. Yet Jonquil's introduction to the human way of life would be very different from Eager's.

"I'm sorry, Jonquil," Eager said. "I wish you could live with a family and learn about the world, as I did. But I can't ask the Bells to look after you."

The ball took on a star shape, Jonquil's favorite guise. "I've done that already," Jonquil said airily.

"Done what?"

"Lived with a family and learnt about the world."

"But you've never left home!" Eager tilted his head again. "I understand. You've practiced with simulations."

"No! A real family," said Jonquil. "I meet them on the go-between. I've been following them for weeks."

"Who are they?" said Eager.

"The Jones family."

"I've never heard of the Jones family," said Eager. A dreadful thought was beginning to form in his mind. He had not lived with the Bells for almost ten years. As he spent less and less time among humans, he was becoming a stranger to their world. Was it possible that his nephew, who had not existed until a few months ago, knew more about people today than he did?

"Where do they live?" Eager asked.

"I'm not sure of the town," said Jonquil. "It's a street like this one. And a very big house. I think that must be because they're a large family and they have lots of friends who are always visiting them."

"Do they have parties?"

"Is a party when you listen to someone's problems?"

"No," said Eager.

"Then they don't have parties," said Jonquil. Star-shaped, he hung in the air above Eager. "So can I stay?"

"There is one small matter," said Eager.

"What's that?"

"Your mother."

The points of the star burst outward and contracted several times.

"Your mother will be worried," Eager said.

"I've thought of that!" Jonquil made another starburst. "She won't even know I've gone. I was going to do what Bobby Jones did when he ran away. He left a big lump under the blankets. But I don't have a bed. So I asked the gobetween what other people did. It told me about two prisoners who collected hair and made it into wigs, which they left on their pillows. But I don't have hair."

"What *did* you do?" said Eager. He imagined Allegra anxiously calling for her son and sending the other robots to search for him.

"I made a hologram of myself," said Jonquil, "and left it in front of the gobetween so it looks as if I'm studying." He floated to the ground and hopped ahead of Eager.

"Your mother will soon realize," said Eager.

"No she won't," said Jonquil. "I did what Lori Jones does whenever she wants to go night surfing with her friends, which she isn't allowed to do. I put a note on the door saying, 'Do not disturb until tomorrow.' "

Eager fell silent; Jonquil did know something of the world after all. "I'll call your mother tomorrow and explain. Meanwhile, you must promise to remain hidden at all times."

"Hidden? Why?"

"Because robots like us are not wanted in the world."

"Why not?"

"Some humans are frightened of robots that can think and feel as they do. They're afraid we might want to harm them."

"That doesn't make sense," said Jonquil.

"I know," said Eager wearily.

Jonquil did a starburst. "Wouldn't they like me if they met me?"

Eager was reminded again of his own excitement at being in the world. If only Jonquil could be spared the truth! But he needed to know. "Humans will be more scared of you than of robots that look like them. For a start, you don't have a head or limbs, like people and insects and animals—you're just one structure that can change shape and even separate into different pieces."

"Isn't that a good thing?" asked Jonquil, sounding unusually timid.

"It's a wonderful thing," said Eager. "But a lot of humans won't understand that."

Jonquil dropped to the ground. "What about the Bells?"

Eager contracted the rings of his legs and bent down until he was level with his nephew. "Listen carefully," he said. "Mr. and Mrs. Bell put themselves in danger by having me to visit. They'll be in worse trouble if you're discovered. It's better that they know nothing about you."

"But—"

"Professor Ogden will be in trouble too."

"All right. I'll camouflage myself. But you'll let me stay?"

"Tonight," said Eager.

"The whole week!" cried Jonquil. "It's a long way back on my own," he added. "I can teach you about the Jones family."

Eager straightened up. "I must talk to your mother."

"Yes! Yes! Yes! Yes!" cried Jonquil, making starbursts all down the road. "Thank you, Uncle Eager."

But Eager wasn't listening. He stood beside a low brick wall gazing up at a lime tree, its branches swollen with yellow blooms. Behind the tree was a house built of glass.

"We're here," he said.

CHAPTER 2

Mrs. Bell placed a vase of flowers on the table and began to tug at the greenery around the lilies.

A green light flickered by the door. "There is someone in the garden," said a silky feminine voice. "Now that it's dark, I am sending out sensors, and I caught the person in my beam."

"We're expecting a visitor," said Mrs. Bell. "It's Eager."

"I did not know," said the voice in what might have been described as a sulky tone.

"He comes this time every year," said Mrs. Bell.

"Well, he's at the door," said the voice.

Mrs. Bell ran into the hallway, shouting for her husband. "Peter! Peter!"

The front door slid open and a slight brown figure entered.

"Look who's here," said the silky voice.

"Hello, house," said Eager. "Hello, Mrs. Bell."

Mrs. Bell clasped his rubbery hands in hers and leant toward him. Taken by surprise, Eager stepped backward against the front door, forgetting that Jonquil had spread himself across his shoulders.

"Oi!" squeaked a voice in his ear.

Eager sprang forward just as Mrs. Bell planted her lips on his cheek. He was overwhelmed with a sensation that he knew to be happiness. This was exactly how Mrs. Bell greeted her grown-up children when they returned home.

Mr. Bell came downstairs. He was wearing a dressing gown over his pajamas. Eager did not expect Mr. Bell to kiss him, and held out his hand to be shaken. But Mr. Bell did a surprising thing too. He clasped both hands around Eager's hand and shook it so heartily that the rubber rings of Eager's arm began to ripple.

"Good to see you, Eager," he said.

"Come into the living room," said Mrs. Bell, leading the way. She stood aside to give Eager a view of the table with the flowers. The robot was aware of the ritual from his previous visits. His eyes went straight to the lilies. "I like the flowers," he said.

Mrs. Bell beamed. "Since I can't offer you food or drink," she said, "I always remember how much you love flowers. At least I can give you those."

"Thank you," said Eager solemnly.

"I don't expect you see much greenery where you are," said Mrs. Bell.

"My home is underground, but there is a view. And I go for walks," said Eager. Every year he reassured her that he was not cut off from nature, but he could tell that she was unconvinced.

"Sit down," said Mr. Bell, "and tell us your news."

Eager went over to the sofa. He remembered not to squash Jonquil against the cushions, and sat on the edge.

"How is Bill?" continued Mr. Bell.

Eager said, "Professor Ogden is very well, or he was when I last saw him. He's away traveling."

"Again?" said Mrs. Bell. "Ever since he left LifeCorp that man hasn't stood still. I know he's a world-famous scientist, but even so . . . I don't suppose it's a holiday this time?"

"I don't think so," said Eager.

"Poor Eager," said Mrs. Bell. "You must miss him. You can't live with the professor, and you can't live with us. It's so cru—"

"Chloe," said her husband warningly.

Mrs. Bell raised a smile. "And how is your sister?"

"Allegra is very well, thank you," said Eager. He couldn't help thinking that she might be less well when she heard about Jonquil.

"I still can't get over there being another robot like you," said Mrs. Bell. "I always think of you as unique."

"He is," said Mr. Bell wryly. "Now, Eager, tell us, what experiments are you working on?"

"Building fault-finding robots," said Eager. "The new technology lets us make smaller and smaller intelligent machines. They can calculate at the speed of light and detect mistakes in other machines." A strong vibration began across Eager's shoulders, as if a thousand tiny fists were pummeling him.

"That's me you're talking about!" his nephew said.

"Have you succeeded in building one yet?" asked Mr. Bell.

Eager hesitated. He didn't want to lie, but he didn't want to tell the truth. Allegra *had* created Jonquil, by reproducing parts of herself. On the other hand, Jonquil had been such an unexpected result that he was not really designed at all.

"Not exactly," said Eager. He felt relieved. He had told the truth after all.

Mr. Bell looked as if he was about to ask another question. Eager changed the subject. "Will I see Charlotte, Gavin and Fleur this week?"

"You certainly will!" said Mrs. Bell. "We're having a family get-together tomorrow. Everyone's coming, except Fleur's husband. He's working on the moon, I'm afraid."

"I thought robots did the work on the moon," said Eager.

"They do, but someone has to supervise them," said Mr. Bell.

"Poor Sam. He's a wonderful scientist, but he doesn't always agree with the other technocrats. . . ."

"A bit like Professor Ogden," said Mrs. Bell.

Eager felt the vibration once more. "Some people sent Brock Jones to the moon, but he ran away in a spaceship!" said Jonquil.

"Yes," said Mr. Bell, "we can't help thinking that Sam's been sent away because he doesn't fit in."

"So why doesn't this man escape?" concluded Jonquil.

"He's not a prisoner," said Eager. Too late, he realized that he had spoken aloud.

"Who? Sam?" said Mr. Bell. "Of course he isn't a prisoner. He's running the robot factory up there."

The activity across Eager's shoulders ceased. Mr. and Mrs. Bell were looking curiously at him. He smiled at them reassuringly.

"Well, it's very late, and we need to go to bed," said Mrs. Bell. "I expect you want to rest too, after that long journey."

"Yes," said Eager. "I must turn down my power and sort out my thoughts."

Mr. and Mrs. Bell stood up. "You can use Gavin's room again," said Mrs. Bell. "I hope that's all right for you."

"Thank you," said Eager.

As soon as they were alone in the bedroom, Jonquil detached himself from Eager's back, changing from a metal shade to his usual straw color. Paper-shaped, he sat slumped on a chair in the corner of the room.

"Welcome to the human world," said Eager.

"It wasn't like the Jones' house," grumbled Jonquil. "Nobody screamed or shouted or fainted. I thought at least the hospital would call to say someone was injured."

"That would be terrible," said Eager. "I wouldn't want an accident to happen to any of the family."

Jonquil bounced into a star shape. "This is my first evening. I expect things will get more interesting tomorrow."

CHAPTER 3

Many kilometers above, a Sorbjet arched its way over Earth. It had taken off like any other aircraft. But once it was high in the sky, a sudden boost of energy sent it soaring into the upper atmosphere, where it entered its suborbital curve. It reached a speed of fourteen thousand kilometers an hour. Any faster, and it would enter orbit.

The sudden thrust had pushed the passengers into their seats. They braced themselves as the Sorbjet continued its climb. Soon they would experience weightlessness.

Finbar had unpacked his lexiscreen, but it lay wordless in his lap. His head was too full of thoughts to read. The knowledge that they were almost in space kept him glued to the window.

It was dark outside and he could see stars, which added to the impression that they had gone far beyond Earth's atmosphere.

"When will there be something more to see?"

His mother glanced at her jinn, which resembled an old-fashioned bracelet. "About now, if I remember rightly."

She patted Finbar's knee. "Don't worry. If we're not invited soon, I'll go and speak to the pilots myself."

He imagined her strolling into the cockpit and introducing herself. One of the pilots was bound to exclaim, "Not *the* Marcia Morris! I love your paintings!" And the next minute Finbar would be having the red-carpet treatment.

His mother was busy reading, and he knew better than to disturb her again. His eyes fell on her new lexiscreen, which was covered in green silk and weighed little more than the fabric itself. Most lexiscreens were flat, but this one opened into two parts like a book. When Marcia wanted to read on, she squeezed gently with her fingers and two whole pages of print appeared.

Finbar watched, enthralled, as the words fluttered into place. The effect was not unlike turning a paper page. His own lexiscreen seemed clumsy by comparison.

"Would you like a drink?"

The attendant was leaning toward him. She had a pretty face, with brown eyes and near-perfect features. Finbar couldn't help stammering, "I . . . I'd like some water, please."

The attendant handed him a covered cup that looked like a child's beaker. "Everything will be weightless in a minute," she said. "Please remember to Velcro this to the chair in front."

"Thank you," said Finbar.

His mother caught his eye. "Finbar," she said warningly. "You know she's an animat. . . ."

"Of course I know." He felt himself blush. "I can still enjoy looking at her, can't I? Like we admire a painting or a view. Isn't that why the manufacturers built her to look nice?"

Marcia ruffled his hair. "As an artist, I can't argue with that. Anyway, you're too young to have your heart broken."

"Oh, really?" he said, and took a long drink.

A buzzer began to sound.

"Ladies and gentlemen," a male voice announced, "we will shortly be experiencing weightlessness. Please return to your seat and ensure that you are strapped in. All personal belongings must be attached by Velcro to your seat. Large bags are to be placed in the lockers. Please call an attendant if you need assistance."

There was a surge of activity in the cabin as the buzzer became louder and more frequent.

"Ladies and gentlemen, the heat-protective shields have been removed from the front of the aircraft. We will soon have a sunlit view of Earth. For your own safety, and that of fellow passengers, please remain in your seats until you are called to the viewing platform. Our flight time is short, and to ensure that everyone has the opportunity to enjoy weightlessness, kindly observe the following: keep aerial gymnastics to a minimum and proceed quickly to the platform. There are rails on the ceiling to assist you. Thank you for your courtesy toward other passengers."

Finbar looked out of the window again. The thin crescent below was showing a wedge of light. He turned excitedly to his mother and his elbow knocked her handbag, releasing it from the net that held it. Marcia caught it before it floated away.

"Finbar!" she said, though she didn't sound as cross as she might have done. She was being especially nice to him on this trip, probably because he'd wanted to stay home.

"Would passengers in seats one to fourteen care to proceed to the viewing platform."

Finbar had been rehearsing his seat number for ages. Thirteen! He released his seat belt and drifted upward. "Mum, this is fantastic! Aren't you coming?"

She smiled up at him. "I'll come later. You may not want to share your experience, the first time."

It was the oddest thing to be in his seat one moment and floating above it the next. Since most of the passengers remained seated, it was easy to imagine that he was still among them and was having an out-of-body experience.

His arms lifted themselves from his sides like spreading wings. But the mechanics of weightlessness proved to be different from swimming and flying. For a start, there was no up or down; there was only "around." He experimented with the best way to turn a somersault. Suddenly, he brushed against the wall. The impact was enough to send him spiraling through the cabin.

"Will the first group of passengers please hurry to the viewing platform," said the male voice.

A woman caught Finbar's eye as she floated past. "Easier said than done," she remarked. She grasped a pole on the ceiling and used it to push herself on to the next pole. He copied her and made his way to the front.

The viewing platform was below the cockpit. Finbar and the other passengers pulled themselves down the narrow steps by holding on to the railings. All he could see were legs and feet.

By now, strangers were talking excitedly to each other. Finbar remembered the standard-class passengers on the lower deck, who had to stay in their seats. His mother had explained that there was too little time to have everyone float through the cabin and there would be chaos. Besides, she added, first-class passengers were paying for the privilege of an extra-fine view.

At the foot of the stairs they floated onto the viewing platform. The chatter died down, followed by deep silence. The sound of twenty jaws hitting the floor, Finbar said to himself.

They were surrounded by glass. There were poles to hold on to. He gripped one, as if otherwise he might propel himself into the star-studded darkness. He looked down to his left and the field of stars came to an abrupt end. He realized that the black patch below them was not the sky, but Earth.

There were lights on Earth, however, spread out like jewels in a crown. He had seen cities from the air before, at night, but they had never sparkled as brightly.

A rim of light appeared, and he saw Earth's outline. He knew it would not be a sphere from that height. But the surface was curved, and bathed in a rainbow of colors!

He caught his breath. Marcia hadn't told him about this.

Gradually, the sun rose over the horizon, drowning out the

spectrum of colors. Now he could see features of a landscape—mountain gorges, forest and desert. He tried to identify different countries, as he'd seen them on a globe, but the rivers and mountains ignored frontiers.

The sea dazzled in the sunlight. A beautiful azure sea, crested with white, it lapped many shores, some of which seemed only a hand span apart. The Mediterranean. Soon he would land in Europe for the first time. His mother still viewed Europe as home, though she hadn't lived there for several years. She was dying to introduce him to old friends and haunts.

Though his own home became further away by the second, he had a sense that the entire earth was his. He understood why his mother had sent him on alone. If she had been beside him, what could he have said to her? Better to be silent, as he marveled at Earth from way above, knowing that it was a tiny sphere, spinning in the universe. Amid the excitement and wonderment, he began to feel something like panic, the sense that he didn't belong up here, and that Earth was a long way away. . . .

CHAPTER 4

"Beautiful, isn't it?"

The speaker, an older man, was holding on to Finbar's pole. His voice was so quiet that Finbar thought he might be speaking to himself, but the man turned to him and smiled.

"Do you know how far up we are?" said Finbar.

"About a hundred kilometers."

"It doesn't sound that much," said Finbar. "Less than an hour's drive in a hovercar!"

"Indeed," said the man. "Whereas a journey to the moon is three hundred and sixty thousand kilometers. Though even that feels surprisingly short."

"Have you been there?" asked Finbar.

"I went once with my work."

"Were you an astronaut?" The man seemed old enough to be retired, though he wasn't as old as his shock of white hair suggested.

The man chuckled. "Goodness me, no! I'm no adventurer. I'm a scientist."

Finbar glanced back at Earth. "It must look incredible from space."

"Yes. It really is a small blue and white marble, against black velvet. . . ." The man smiled again. "Of course, you may not have seen a marble."

Finbar gazed at the wash of a ship, slicing the sea. "I've played marbles," he said. "My dad taught me the old games—cards, real chess. He's a traddy. Traditionalist," he added, seeing the man looked puzzled.

"Is he traveling with you?" said the man.

Finbar shook his head. "He's on retreat, as he calls it. He goes somewhere quiet, up into the mountains. He's a poet." He paused. "What was it like in space? Did it change you?"

"I'm not sure I was changed," the man said thoughtfully. "But I think I was improved! I felt much closer to my real self—the better me." He smiled. "I had an extraordinary sense of peace up there, as if everything were right with the universe. And all the things we worry about on Earth suddenly seemed petty and ridiculous." He gave a sigh. "I wish everyone could go into space. Then we might all feel the same way and live in harmony at last."

"When they build a sky-hook . . . ," Finbar said eagerly. "You know, a cable that goes from the earth to a satellite in orbit—then we could all take the lift up. 'Which floor, sir?' "

"Space, please." The man and Finbar laughed together. "Well, carbon nanotubes are marvelous things, but the engineers haven't yet worked out how to make this cable." The man sounded as if he knew what he was talking about.

"Perhaps there's another way," said Finbar hesitantly. "I mean, we're finding out more and more about the universe, aren't we?"

"We are. At the same time, we're finding out more about smaller universes. We can manipulate matter as tiny as atoms. I mentioned carbon nanotubes. As you probably know, it takes fifty thousand of them to cover the width of a hair! Think what worlds we're opening up! The same thing is happening with space exploration."

"So what do you think will happen?"

The man shook his head. "I would like to think our consciousness would expand too. You see, we are extraordinary beings. Life and consciousness are the greatest mysteries of all. Yet we act as if they were quite ordinary."

Finbar's father said similar things in his poems, but Finbar wasn't used to hearing them in conversation, especially not from a stranger floating in the air. He couldn't help smiling.

"Of course, you're young. You don't want to think about these things," said the man in a friendly way.

"No! I'm interested," said Finbar. "Do you know a lot about consciousness?"

The man said, half to himself, "No more than anyone. Yet I've been traveling the world for months talking about it." His tone brightened. "Have you ever looked in a mirror and tried to see what others see?"

"When they look at me, you mean?" said Finbar. "It doesn't really work, does it? Because when you're with someone, your face does all sorts of expressions you don't know about, and the minute you look in a mirror, you lose the expressions."

There was a twinkle in the man's eye. "That's exactly it," he said. "It's the same with consciousness, isn't it? We can never capture the moment. As soon as we say 'now I'm aware of myself,' it becomes meaningless. That's why we'll never understand consciousness. The answer is within us, but we can't hold a mirror to it."

Finbar thought, "I know what he means, but it's still mind-boggling."

The viewing platform was getting crowded, and the man moved away to let someone take his place. He said, "I'll leave you to the spectacle. Thank you for our most interesting conversation."

CHAPTER 5

Finbar stayed for some time as people came and went. He watched a flotilla of sailing boats on the sea. . . . He glanced at his jinn. The flight was nearly at an end. He had crossed half the world in the time it took to eat lunch! To think of all the people, houses, trees, plants, animals, mountains and blades of grass he had literally hopped over. Pulling himself up the stairs, he passed his mother, horizontal, on her way to the platform.

He laughed and waved. Back in the cabin, he tried to swim his way to his seat. There were more people floating than before, and someone bumped into him.

"Hey!" He rubbed his shoulder. He felt so cushioned in weightlessness that he didn't expect to feel pain.

The offender was a sullen-looking boy.

Finbar tended to be shy; his mother said it was because he was an only child. She was always encouraging him to make friends, though he told her he liked his own company. But now he was bursting to talk, and a midair collision was an introduction of sorts.

"Hello, I'm Finbar."

The boy took his time. "Hello." No expression.

"Isn't it amazing?" said Finbar, barely above a whisper. He had the feeling that if he spoke normally he wouldn't be able to control his voice; it would rise to an ecstatic shout and attract everyone's attention.

The boy stared at him.

"All this! The earth," said Finbar. Still the boy did not respond.

"Thinks I'm mad." Embarrassed, Finbar steered his body around.

"Haven't seen it," the boy said.

Finbar looked back. The boy jerked his head toward the staircase. "No windows down there. No viewing platform either."

Now that he'd been on the viewing platform, Finbar thought it was unfair not to let everyone go. No wonder there had been no answering excitement in the boy's eyes.

"Take my place!" he said. "Go down to the viewing platform."

The boy showed emotion for the first time. Astonishment, pleasure . . . his pale skin became flushed, even. Then he shook his head. "Not allowed."

"But I am. That's what I'm saying—pretend to be me. Finbar Khan is my name."

"And if they stop me?"

"Take my jinn." Finbar peeled it from his wrist. "Tell it to say my ticket number if anyone tries to stop you. Get cross and say you don't expect that sort of treatment in first class."

The boy reached for the jinn eagerly. Finbar made sure that he had hold of it before letting go, afraid it might float away.

As he put it on, the boy's eyes glinted, then became dull again. "The jinn will betray me, won't it?" he said. "Soon as I look at it, it'll go on the alert because I'm not you."

Finbar frowned. He'd forgotten this.

The boy had taken off the jinn. He silently handed it back.

"Wait!" Finbar used the tip of his finger to punch the small buttons at the side of the screen. "Look straight," he said, holding up the jinn to the boy's eyes. "There. Now your retinogram has replaced mine. The jinn will think you're me when you face the screen. The override will only last for ten minutes—" He broke off at the sound of the buzzer.

"Ladies and gentlemen, in ten minutes, weightlessness will cease and we will begin the descent to Earth. Please strap yourselves securely in your seat."

"Hurry!" cried Finbar. "You should just make it." He called after the boy, "Keep away from a woman in a blue dress. That's my mum. She might get upset if she hears you saying you're me!"

While he waited, Finbar sat down in the restaurant, hooking his feet under the bars of the chair to stop himself drifting away.

Within six minutes, the boy was back, looking like a different person. Finbar could have sworn that he was floating with a swagger, or its equivalent. He handed the jinn to Finbar, who slipped it on. It was good to feel the familiar band in place again.

"Well?" said Finbar.

"No one stopped me."

"I didn't mean that." The boy's eyes were shining: he must be dying to say something.

"Is that really your mum? The woman in the blue dress?"

Finbar gaped. He had just given the boy a view of the planet and all he wanted to talk about was his *mum*? "Yes, that's her. But what about Earth?"

"Oh, yeah, it was great," said the boy.

"Good," said Finbar coldly. The boy couldn't have sounded more bored if he'd tried.

"Ladies and gentlemen, please return to your seats immediately." Finbar undid his belt and drifted out of the restaurant chair.

"Your mum," called the boy, "what does she do?"

"She's an artist," Finbar said. The boy kept his eyes on him. "She paints, sculpts . . . that sort of thing."

The boy pulled himself down the stairs, leaving Finbar seething. He reminded himself that the boy had every right not to be impressed by the view of Earth. But he might at least have said thank you. "Ungrateful moonrock!" Finbar thought. He shook his head. Why was he so angry?

The boy had been so pleased at the chance to visit the viewing platform. "That's why I'm cross," thought Finbar. "I expected him to come back as excited as I was and talk about it."

He seized the handrail on the stairs to go after the boy. He would ask him why he hadn't enjoyed the view. . . .

A hand held Finbar back. He swung round to face the brown-eyed stewardess.

She smiled fetchingly. "You must return to your seat."

For the first time he noticed a steeliness in her eyes. He indulged in a final somersault and dived into his place.

Gradually his annoyance lifted. Maybe the boy just didn't want to talk, or he would have got into trouble if he didn't hurry back to his family. . . . The boy. He hadn't even told Finbar his name.

"Are you all right, darling?" His mother was upside down, trying to right herself onto her seat.

Finbar avoided her eyes. "I'm fine."

CHAPTER 6

Meanwhile, at the Bells', the blinds opened in Gavin's room, letting sunlight pour in. Refreshed, Eager turned his power to its normal level and stood up from the floor.

"Jonquil?"

No reply. Eager looked around the bedroom. It was a lot tidier than it had been when Gavin lived there, but many of his things were still in place—pictures, books and a stack of microchips and sensors in a transparent box.

Eager peered into the box. His nephew might feel at home there. "Jonquil?' No answer. He must have slipped out under the door during the night. Eager left the bedroom and went up a small flight of stairs to the top of the house. He found his nephew there, star-shaped, opposite a large gobetween screen.

"Hello, Uncle Eager. I've been finding out about the Joneses."

"How is the family?"

"Devastated," said Jonquil. "Mr. Jones' best friend stole all his money, and Lori Jones was struck down by a hoverbus."

"Is she alive?" said Eager.

"Hanging by a thread."

"That's dreadful. I'm sorry to hear it. Her parents must be very worried."

"They are," said Jonquil. "Mrs. Jones canceled her hair appointment."

Eager looked at the gobetween screen. "And all this happened yesterday?"

"Yes," said Jonquil. "I told you—things happen to the Joneses."

"Loss is very painful," said Eager. "I hope your friend Lori recovers." He walked to the door. "I'm going downstairs to prepare breakfast for Mr. and Mrs. Bell. I used to make it for the family when I lived here."

Jonquil hopped downstairs after his uncle. "I like breakfast. The arguments are always good, first thing in the morning."

No one was up. "I'll make pancakes. Hello," Eager said as he stepped into the pantry to fetch flour.

The pantry did not respond.

He took milk and eggs from the fridge. When the batter was ready he carried the jug to the kitchen table. Halfway there something flapped in front of his right eye. Eager held up a hand to brush it aside. The flapping object moved to his left eye, and rapidly from eye to eye, avoiding Eager's hand each time.

Eager set down the jug and rubbed both eyes. As he withdrew his hands he noticed a pair of wings perched on his left forefinger. Even his acute eyesight could barely see them. He raised the finger to his eye and saw, not a winged insect, but a mass of tiny hairs, gently vibrating.

Eager felt alarm. The fibers that made up Jonquil were coated in thousands of these cilia, like the hairs on a leaf. Some of them could detach themselves from Jonquil and form different shapes. They were too few to create speech, and their limited power meant they could not function for long on their own.

"Where is he?" cried Eager. The wing-shaped cilia flew over to the fridge, where they beat against the door.

Eager flung open the fridge. A ball rolled off the top shelf.

He managed to catch the icy bundle before it hit the ground.

"Jonquil!" he cried. His nephew's curiosity had no limits. Eager must have shut the door on him, but the microscopic cilia had passed through the gap.

Jonquil was still. Eager cradled his nephew in his arms and looked around for something to wrap him in. As he searched for a towel, he heard the sound of the kitchen door. He pulled open the oven and threw Jonquil inside, shutting the door after him.

"Morning, Eager," said Mrs. Bell.

The robot turned to face her. She was in her dressing gown.

"Good morning, Mrs. Bell. I was just making pancakes."

"That's very thoughtful of you," said Mrs. Bell, walking toward him. Eager stayed with his back to the oven.

"Excuse me, Eager, I just need to talk to the oven."

Eager moved aside.

"Oven—level six," said Mrs. Bell in a clear voice. She went over to the kettle. "I'm cooking for tonight and it's always good to do things in advance, isn't it?"

Eager bent down to the height of the oven. "Level one," he whispered.

"Make up your mind," said the oven.

"What was that?" said Mrs. Bell.

"Nothing," said Eager. "Mrs. Bell, I'll make tea for you."

"Thank you, Eager. I'll go and have my shower in the meantime."

Mrs. Bell took an agonizingly long time to cross the kitchen.

At last the door closed behind her. Eager threw open the oven and scooped out Jonquil with both hands. The lacy fibers were warm.

"I don't think it's cooked yet," said the oven. "If you ask me, it would be better boiled and mashed."

"Moiled and bashed?" said a sleepy-sounding voice.

Eager carried Jonquil over to the worktop. He weighed next to nothing. The top of the ball was slightly squashed and the fibers had lost their golden glow. Eager was reminded of a meringue. As he opened a window to let in some cool air, he recalled the time, many years ago, when he had looked after the Bells' baby, Charlotte. He had to keep an eye on her at all times. She was always exploring the world and had no sense of its perils. Just like Jonquil. But Jonquil was fully formed. He could do things and go places in ways that little Charlotte could not. He was—Eager searched for the word—independent.

"I shall have to send you home," Eager said. Home! Home was where Allegra would soon discover that Jonquil was missing. He must call his sister. But he needed Jonquil to do that.

"Jonquil, wake up!" he cried. "Wake up!"

The ball didn't move. Eager took it in his hands and went upstairs, pausing on the top landing to make sure no one was about. He heard a shower running and Mr. Bell singing. Eager hurried on to the gobetween room.

■ ■ ■ ■ ■

"Did you notice Eager last night?" said Mrs. Bell, coming into the bedroom. "I thought he was . . . preoccupied."

Mr. Bell stroked his chin. "Seemed all right to me."

"He was a bit jumpy this morning," said Mrs. Bell. "In the kitchen. I hope he isn't worrying about Professor Ogden."

"He's probably excited to be back with us. It can't be fun for him, shut away the rest of the time."

"I wish there was something we could do."

"So do I, Chloe," said Mr. Bell gently. "But Bill says that all we can do is wait. I'm inclined to agree with our professor friend. The world is just not ready for robots like Eager."

"When will it ever be?" sighed Mrs. Bell.

CHAPTER 7

Jonquil lay curled into a ball on the floor of the go-between room. Eager stood helplessly beside him, imagining Allegra calling for her lost son. He began to consider using the gobetween, but Professor Ogden had told him never to ask the gobetween to connect him to home. "They'll find you if you do." Eager wasn't too sure who "they" were, but he remembered the professor's look and tone: the consequences would be grave. The other robots had received the same instruction. But what if Allegra, in her alarm, ignored the warning and called Eager to tell him that Jonquil had disappeared?

Eager tried to think. "How can I speak to Allegra without asking the gobetween to connect me?"

In a flash, the answer came to him. Eager did not need the whole of Jonquil to help him: he needed his cilia! His nephew was a fault-finding robot, and the cilia were the part of Jonquil that went into a machine to correct any faults. Eager shot out of the room and ran down the stairs, bumping into Mr. Bell. "Sorry, Mr. Bell," he shouted over his shoulder.

No sign of the cilia-wings beside the fridge. Eager looked high and low. He got down on his knees and, with his face close to the ground, plowed up and down the kitchen floor. At last he spotted them. He used a forefinger to nudge them gently onto the palm of his hand. A slight fluttering showed that they still had some power.

He whispered, "I need to send a message on the gobetween. Can you connect me?"

A tremor passed through the wings. Eager ran back up the stairs and entered the gobetween room.

"Jonquil?" Still no response. Eager took the cilia to the gobetween's control panel.

"I need to speak to Allegra," he told them.

As he spoke, the cilia-wings began to dissolve. Within a picosecond, nothing remained in the palm of his hand, or so it appeared. The cilia had joined up, end to end, to form a long filament. But a single cilium was too minuscule for even Eager's eye to see. He waited until he judged that they had entered the gobetween, and lowered his hand.

His thoughts turned to Allegra. All the years that he had lived with the Bells—though he had tried not to think about it—he had longed to know a robot like himself. When he returned briefly to Professor Ogden's house, the professor had led him to his old room under the eaves. There he had seen a robot just like him. She was slighter in build and her face was more oval than round, but there was no doubt that she was an EGR3.

"Your sister," Professor Ogden had said. Or perhaps Eager

had imagined these words, for he had known at once who she was.

Now, on the gobetween, Allegra was looking at him with quiet surprise. Obviously, she hadn't discovered Jonquil's absence yet. "Hello, Eager. Did Professor Ogden tell you to use the gobetween?"

Eager tilted his head. Allegra's experience of life was very different from his own. She'd never lived in the confusing, unpredictable world of humans. Though she lived with robots that could think for themselves, they generally behaved in an orderly way. Things had changed since the arrival of Jonquil, but even Jonquil had never gone so far as to run away from home before. Eager wished he didn't have to disturb Allegra's calm.

"It's all right," he said. "Jonquil connected us." He tailed off.

"Jonquil? But he's here."

"Ah," said Eager.

"I just saw him," said Allegra. "He's studying."

"That was a hologram. Jonquil's with me. He hid in the pod last night."

"With you? You mean he's *out there?*" Allegra looked over her shoulder at the window behind her. She never ventured outside the compound, and Eager knew she was afraid of the world beyond.

"He's all right," said Eager.

Allegra faced Eager. "Where is he?" she cried.

At that moment the ball began to unfurl. "Mother," said Jonquil faintly.

"Jonquil!" said Allegra, her eyes alighting on him. "You must return home at once."

"But I've come to be with Uncle Eager. I want to learn . . ." He broke off. "There's something missing," he said weakly.

Eager knelt beside his nephew. "A bit of you is in the go-between, connecting us to your mother," he said.

"I need to come back," said Jonquil, almost inaudibly.

Eager jumped up. "I'm sorry, Allegra. We must shut down now. I'll call you later."

"When? When?" cried Allegra.

Eager had never seen his sister flustered before. He stared at her with interest until he remembered: Jonquil! "Tomorrow morning," he shouted. "Gobetween, switch off!"

The screen went dark.

He went over to the control panel. How was he going to get the cilia out of there? Would they hear him calling?

"I'm all right, Uncle Eager," said Jonquil. "I came out as soon as the job was done." When Eager looked round he was golden, performing starbursts. "I'm back together again!"

He posed in midair before crumpling into a heap on the floor.

Eager ran over and was reassured to see that Jonquil was still vibrating. "You need to rest. The heat of the oven has destabilized your energy. Stay here for today."

"But . . . ," said Jonquil weakly.

"I'll come up and see you when I can," said Eager.

CHAPTER 8

Finbar stepped off the Sorbjet and into the tunnel that led to the airport. In these stark, familiar surroundings, it was hard to believe that he had actually been to the edge of space. He wished he could have landed on a vast plain, surrounded by vegetation under a blue sky. He wanted to take gulps of fresh air and enjoy the natural sights that he'd seen from above.

Instead he looked down on a smooth gray floor, scuffed with foot marks. He stared at the prints for several seconds, thinking of the people who had made them. Did they even realize that they had left this mark on Earth?

He caught up with his mother on the walkway to the arrivals hall. She had a small cabin bag that shuffled along ahead of her and bleeped annoyingly whenever it moved too far from its owner.

"Why don't I carry it?" said Finbar.

"Oh, leave it," said his mother. "At least it isn't tripping people up."

In the arrivals hall they joined the queue for identity control.

Finbar's eyes darted everywhere as he searched for the boy. If only he could ask him what had happened on the viewing platform and why seeing Earth hadn't impressed him. Finbar scanned the queue. No boy, but he did see the white-haired man waiting at the head of the queue for a retinogram. The officials ushered him toward the retinogram machine. No one else in the queue received such attention.

Finbar turned to ask his mother about the man. If he was at all famous, she was bound to know him. But Marcia was busy speaking to someone on her jinn. ". . . We're at the airport now. . . . Tonight? That would be wonderful. . . . Will Gavin be there? . . . We'll meet you at the house. . . ."

Marcia turned to Finbar. "My friend Fleur has invited us to a family supper. . . . What are you staring at?"

The man had disappeared among the crowd.

"Just someone I met on board," Finbar said.

They were next in line for a retinogram. They walked toward separate machines.

"Jinn, please," said a voice. An arm from the machine held out a hand to receive Finbar's jinn. "Khan, Finbar David," said the machine.

An optical sensor on a longer arm adjusted itself to Finbar's height. "Do not blink," said the voice. The sensor passed in front of his eyes. "Identity confirmed."

He caught up with his mother. "Our luggage is ready," she said, glancing at her jinn-bracelet. As they hurried toward the baggage hall, Finbar looked back at the queue. No boy.

A long white hovercar waited for them outside the airport. They were guided to it by Marcia's jinn, which buzzed at different pitches until they located it. An animat-porter loaded their luggage in the back.

Marcia sat in the driving seat and punched a code into the control panel. The hovercar rose from the ground. "I thought we'd go via the center," she said as she guided it onto the main road. "I'd like to show you some of the city before we get to the hotel."

The route was lined with buildings. Many of them seemed centuries old to Finbar. He tried to imagine the people who had lived and worked in them. "What would they say if they saw us traveling off the ground?" he wondered. "Long ago, we'd have been burnt as witches," he decided. They drove past a large park with playing fields and cafés. Beyond it was an endless row of shops, fronted by billscreens almost as high as the buildings.

"Big and brash, isn't it?" said his mother. "It was always a bit like this, but I hardly came here when I was your age, because the city was for people without jobs, outsiders, eccentrics. When the social barriers between the city people and the rest of us came down it turned out the city people were wonderfully creative. They had the best music, movies, theaters and gobey-halls . . . That's why I went to art school here."

They were caught in traffic behind a hoverbus dropping off passengers and a delivery pod overtaking it. A bicycle pulled out behind the hovercar. "I'm taking the next turning!" said Marcia impatiently.

"Whittaker and Co!" she cried as they passed a large store. "My favorite shop. Famous for its displays."

A waterfall of chairs and sofas, not water, spilled from the roof of the building onto the forecourt. His mother drew up at the side of the road. The hovercar sank down. "Come on," said Marcia, opening her door.

Finbar joined her at the foot of the cascade. The chairs and sofas tumbled perilously downward, and he kept losing sight of them in the foam. "What is it?"

"The new generation of billscreen," said his mother. She seized his hand and pulled him under the waterfall.

He told himself: "There's nothing to hit me—no water and no furniture." But he couldn't help flinching. Marcia stood beside him. From the corner of his eye he saw her raise her head, as if to feel gushing water against her face. He steeled himself to do the same, but it looked as if rods were falling on him, and he grew dizzy.

He ran out. "That's enough!" he shouted.

His mother lowered her head and smiled at him. He reminded himself that her parents had been technocrats and she'd grown up with the latest technology. Nothing surprised her. By comparison, Finbar had led a sheltered life.

CHAPTER 9

Eager was slicing carrots in the kitchen. His nephew was still resting upstairs. "I wish I could tell the Bells about Jonquil," Eager thought. When he lived with the Bells he had kept his guide, the luminous ball Sphere, a secret, until one day he discovered that Gavin knew about Sphere too. It would be such a relief to share the knowledge of Jonquil with someone. . . .

But Sphere was serene, independent and very wise; Professor Ogden had said that it was a higher form of consciousness. Sphere could look after itself. Whereas Jonquil was hotheaded and needed constant attention. "It isn't fair to burden the Bells with the secret," Eager said to himself.

A green light by the door flickered. "Just like old times, you working in the kitchen," said the house.

"Yes," said Eager.

The feminine voice continued, "You'll need more food than that. Fleur has invited her old friend Marcia Morris to supper. Marcia's son, Finbar, is coming too."

"I should like to see Marcia again," said Eager. "She used to come here a lot when I lived with the Bells. Mrs. Bell told me she went to another country and had a baby, just after Fleur was married."

"She's a famous artist now," said the house. "I think her paintings strike an interesting balance between the conceptual and the—"

Mrs. Bell came into the kitchen. "It's turning into a party."

"I know," said Eager. "Marcia is coming, with her son."

"And Gavin just called," said Mrs. Bell. "He's bringing a friend. Her name's Molly."

This was not the first time, over the years, that Mrs. Bell had mentioned a friend of Gavin's in unusual tones. Though she spoke airily, there was a hint of an emotion in her voice that Eager could never quite define. Was it excitement, or frustration, or pleasure, or amusement even? He looked closely at Mrs. Bell's face, but her expression was unchanged and offered no clue to the mystery. "Molly," he said softly. It was a new name to him, and he wanted to remember it.

"All we need now," said Mrs. Bell, "is for Charlotte to invite the college liveball team." While Eager was deciding whether this was a likely event, Mrs. Bell disappeared into the pantry. She reemerged, her arms full of vegetables. "She's only coming tonight to see you. If you weren't here, she'd just call us on the gobey as usual."

She smiled at the robot and glanced away quickly. But a look had passed between them that left Eager feeling regretful.

"I miss you all when I'm away," he said.

Mrs. Bell nodded. "We miss you too. Fancy banning robots like you! I was saying to Peter earlier, if only the world would come to its senses." She looked sad for a moment. "I'm glad you have a family of your own—Allegra, and the other robots. I would hate to think of you being alone."

"At least I can visit you," said Eager.

"Even that isn't straightforward," said Mrs. Bell, sighing. It was unlike her to be so despondent. "Take tonight. There'll be strangers here, not to mention Fleur's daughter, Ju. She's still too young to be told about you. We must be careful."

Eager said brightly, "Don't worry, Mrs. Bell. I shall keep in the background like a house robot, and the visitors will hardly notice me."

CHAPTER 18

Ju left the learning center, jubilant. A story that had taken her weeks to write had been a big hit in class, and in the afternoon she'd beaten her personal best in swimming.

She walked along with her best friend, Luisa. "How about going to a gobeyhall tonight?" Luisa said.

"I can't," said Ju. "Family party at my grandparents'. Maybe next week."

They reached the gate and the porter, an animat, came out of his box. "Are you leaving?"

"Yes," said Luisa solemnly.

"How are you getting home?"

Luisa giggled. "Flying."

The porter's expression went blank for an instant.

"Taking the hoverbus," said Luisa, raising her eyebrows at Ju.

"I shall monitor you until you are safely on the hoverbus," said the porter. He turned to Ju. "And you?"

"I'm walking."

"Would you like to hire an animat to escort you?" he said.

"No, I wouldn't," said Ju.

"Are you old enough to walk home on your own?"

"It isn't far," said Ju. "Anyway, I'm sixteen."

This was absurd. Though she was tall for her age, anyone could tell that she wasn't sixteen. She didn't have the figure, for a start. But the animat walked back to the box without another word.

Ju and Luisa went out of the gate. "Why was he fussing?" said Luisa.

"I don't know," said Ju. "Perhaps there's been a security alert. But don't worry, he'll be monitoring you."

Luisa giggled again. "My mum said she used to have a robot with her all the time."

"So did mine," said Ju. "It spoilt her for life. She can't cook, can't cross roads on her own, her bedroom's a mess. . . ."

"You're exaggerating," said Luisa. "Your mum's a food technologist!"

"Doesn't mean she can cook. She understands nutrition and how to design robochefs. But ask her to boil an egg . . ."

The hoverbus swept into the level of the bus stop. The curved double doors opened and Luisa climbed on. She waved. "See you Monday."

Ju zigzagged her way through side streets. Animats were everywhere—sweeping, painting, lugging rubbish from houses and gardens. Ju turned into the main road, a tumult of sound and movement. She fumbled inside her sleeve to check that her ID shield was on. Billscreens continued to flash, sing jingles and roll out their sales patter, but her ID shield meant that none of it was directed at her. She crossed and slipped thankfully into the backstreets once more.

At the end of a cul-de-sac was a tall austere building. It had been built of concrete at the end of the last century, with no decoration to relieve its gray exterior. Once it had housed offices, but now it was a dance school. Its tucked-away location meant cheap rents, no neighbors to disturb and plenty of space for studios.

Ju stopped a few meters away, looking and listening. During the week all kinds of music burst out of the building, and you could see heads bobbing up and down in the windows. But everyone had left for the weekend.

Suddenly Ju felt as empty as the building. She walked round to the side where a glass lift clung to the wall. She watched the ground recede as she rose, and the lift shot beyond the height of the other buildings.

Ju stepped out onto the rooftop. In the middle was a single-story house, with an open space in front of it. As the weather was fine, a table and chairs had been left outside. Tubs of flowers formed the edge of the terrace and behind them were railings, interwoven with sweet peas and honeysuckle.

The entrance door recognized Ju and let her in. To the right were a kitchen, bedroom and bathroom. The other side of the hallway was one large living space, flanked by windows that formed the front of the house. One corner was screened off to make a bedroom for Ju.

Her parents had bought the flat when they married. It was ideal for two people who went out a lot. For three people who liked to relax at home, it was a squash.

"Hello, Ju," said a male voice. The gobetween. "How was your day at the learning center?"

She kicked off her shoes and watched them slide across the rubber floor. "OK. Busy, though. Everyone and their dog was there."

She went up to the kitchen door. It slid open, and she stepped into the empty room.

Lately she'd begun to convince herself that she would come home and find her parents together. They would look round as she walked in, their smiles growing wider to include her. "Guess who's here!" her mum would say. Her dad would bound to Ju and sweep her into a bear hug.

No one was there, of course. Her mum was at work as usual, and her dad was three hundred and sixty thousand kilometers away. She had to stop her fantasies!

A light flashed beside the door. "Do many dogs attend the learning center?" said the deep voice.

"Dogs?" said Ju. "That's a ridiculous question—even for a gobetween. You know what a dog is."

"You said it first," said the gobetween.

"It was a joke," said Ju. She began to open cupboards and peer inside.

"Don't you have any studying to do?"

"I'll do it this weekend." She went over to the fridge.

"If you're hungry, I hope you will eat properly."

Ju frowned, her head in the fridge. "Have I ever told you you're worse than any parent?"

There was a pause.

"I'm trying to remember," said the gobetween.

"Don't bother," said Ju. She closed the fridge door.

"I will happily advise you on nutrition," said the gobetween. "Have you tested your blood today? You're looking peaky."

"Thanks a lot," said Ju. All the same, she went over to a narrow black box beside the sink. Her mother had just installed it and made Ju promise to use it. Ju's father was the cook of the family and in his absence her mother worried about Ju's health.

Ju thrust her hand into the box's opening, quickly before there was time to think about what was coming. "Ow!" she cried as the needle pricked her index finger.

"Painful?" said the gobetween.

Ju went into the living area and over to the big glass windows. "Open," she said, and walked onto the terrace. The sun was still warm. But the silence was eerie. At least when the dance school was closed at the weekend, she had her mum for company. She went back inside.

"Your food is ready," said the gobetween.

In the kitchen, Ju retrieved a green drink from a dispenser beneath the black box. It had the consistency of frog spawn, in Ju's opinion. Dark strands appeared when she shook the cup. "What is this?"

"It includes extract of spinach, mackerel, apples and linseed oil—apparently you're lacking in vitamins, omega three oils—"

"I don't really want to know," said Ju.

"Fleur is home," said the gobetween.

Ju rushed to greet her mother at the front door, holding out the cup.

"Hi, Mum. Look, I'm using the machine."

"I'm pleased to hear it." Her mother hung up her jacket.

"How was your day?"

"I beat my freestyle time," said Ju.

"Well done," said her mother absently. "Listen, I've had some exciting news. Guess who's coming—"

Ju gripped her mum's arm. "Dad! They're sending him home!" she breathed.

"Oh, Ju, I'm sorry!" Her mum placed her hands on Ju's shoulders. "That was thoughtless of me. I was talking about Marcia—you know, my old friend. She's here, and her son's with her. You remember Finbar, don't you?"

"No," said Ju.

Her mother dropped her arms. "I've invited them to Gran and Grandpa's this evening. It'll be wonderful to see her again. Talking on the gobey is never the same as spending time with someone."

"It's better than nothing," said Ju. Her tone was defiant. Fleur put an arm around Ju and pulled her close. "You're thinking of Dad, aren't you? You're right, we're very lucky to have gobey contact with him." She sighed. "I love these family get-togethers, but they always remind me of how far away Sam is."

"I know."

"But it won't be forever. A couple of months and he'll be back," said her mum, giving a strained smile.

She looked at her jinn. "Now go and drink your snack. He'll be calling soon, and you've only got a couple of hours to get it down."

"Very funny," said Ju.

CHAPTER 11

"Ju, your dad's here," her mum's voice called to her.

For a second, Ju thought that her father might really be there, looking for her with those keen eyes, which she used to believe could read her thoughts. She ran from the kitchen into the living area and saw him as clear as anything on the large go-between screen.

"Ju," he cried, opening his arms wide. "Big hug."

Ju snatched up the touch-mantle that her mum had left beside the screen and wrapped it around herself. The mesh of wires and sensors sat lightly on her shoulders. Her dad folded his arms around his own body and Ju felt the pressure of his hug. She smiled.

"Hi, Dad."

"How are you?" he said, relaxing his arms. The absence of pressure was a jolt to Ju. "Your mum tells me you're using her nutrition machine. In fact, I can see from here"—he leant forward—"your eyes are sparkling from all those vitamins; your hair is shining. As for your nose . . ."

"Dad, I'm not a dog," said Ju. "Though you should have heard what the gobey said today. It thought dogs might go to the learning center."

They laughed. Her father said, "But don't forget, we're making so much progress in science, the gobetween has a job to keep up with us. For all it knows, we may well have bred a dog that loves astrophysics."

Ju smiled wanly. She liked to hear her dad talk in this way, but not when time was precious.

"What did you do at the learning center today?" he said.

She told him about her story and the new swimming time.

"Well done!" her dad said. "You know, that's something I miss—plunging into a cool pool. . . . "

"I wish you could—" Ju began.

"But guess what?" Her dad smiled. "I've just programmed the running machine to show the streets around home. Short on greenery, but it's fun to remember what the place looks like."

Ju bit her lip. She was never sure whether her dad was positive for her benefit, or because he really was happy on the moon.

"Wouldn't you prefer to be a tourist?" she said. "Stay for a few days and then fly home again?"

"Sometimes." He grinned. "But you should see what's planned for the latest tourists. They're here to play 'Stars in Space.' Get it? It's a pun because they're well-known people— singers, actors, liveball players. . . . You can watch it on the gobey this weekend."

"I'd rather see you. Not playing games, just being where you are."

"My work is top-security, remember. Though goodness knows why: we're only breaking up moonrocks." His expression changed. "I'm going to the far side this weekend. I'm picking up the people from the listening station and dropping off the new crew."

Her face fell. She remembered the last time her dad had made the trip. "So we won't be hearing from you?" she said, trying to keep her voice light.

" 'Fraid not. The far side has no radio contact with Earth."

"I hate it when there's no contact," said Ju. "It's as if you've floated away into space."

"Ju, it's not as bad as it sounds. If there's any problem, the crew can quickly hook up to the orbital satellite and send a message to Earth, or the moon base. The radio link is only turned off so that the crew can listen out for signals from space."

"Well, if you do hear from any extraterrestrials, I've got a message for them."

"What's that?"

"Send my dad home."

He laughed. "If you don't hear from me Sunday night, you'll know I'm on my way! I'd better go and get ready now."

He folded his arms around himself and Ju felt the embrace of the mantle once more.

"OK, Dad," she said. "Enjoy your trip."

"You enjoy yourself too. Bye, Ju. I love you."

"I love you, Dad. Bye-bye . . ."

Her voice tailed off as the screen became dark. Ju sat silently for a moment before pulling the touch-mantle from her shoulders.

CHAPTER 12

Later that evening Ju and Fleur took the hoverbus to the suburbs where Mr. and Mrs. Bell lived. They walked along Wynston Avenue and had just reached the bend when a sleek white hovercar glided past. Through the window, Ju recognized her mum's friend Marcia.

"Fleur!" Marcia jumped down from the car.

While they hugged, Ju turned her attention to the boy stepping onto the pavement. He looked a lot like his mother, though darker-skinned. He was a bit shorter than Ju.

"This is Finbar," said Marcia, drawing him toward her. "And, of course, you're—"

"Ju," said Fleur hastily.

"I've never understood why you don't use your full name. It's so pretty," said Marcia to Ju. "Is it because you couldn't say it when you were little?"

Ju shrugged. She only knew that she liked one name and not the other.

Marcia kissed her on the cheek. The smell of her perfume was overwhelming. She said, "Well, it's wonderful to meet you properly at last, Ju."

Inside the house Mr. and Mrs. Bell rushed to greet the visitors. Eager kept in the kitchen, though he was delighted to hear Fleur's voice again. He recognized Marcia's voice too, though it sounded different after all these years. Their talk reminded Eager of when they were younger and their nonstop chatter had filled the house.

As they made their way to the atrium, where Eager had helped put out cold drinks, he heard Mrs. Bell say, "If you feel tired, Finbar, just go upstairs for a lie-down. There are plenty of spare beds."

Eager froze. A visitor wandering to the top of the house? He waited until the hallway was silent before bounding up the stairs to the gobetween room.

No Jonquil.

Eager called his name. Jonquil might still be too weak to respond. Being put in the oven had drained his energy. Eager felt the chairs tentatively, in case Jonquil was lying on one, camouflaged. He went down the stairs to Gavin's room, repeating the process—patting the bed, scrutinizing the carpet and calling gently for his nephew.

It was no good. Eager could hardly go through the entire house like this; he was needed in the kitchen. He'd go downstairs and think what to do. In the meantime, Jonquil must surely return to the gobetween room.

As he walked down, Gavin Bell arrived: Eager could hear his

laughter. He wished he could go and greet him, but Gavin wouldn't be alone. As he crossed to the kitchen, the front door slid open and a figure propelled itself toward him. "Eager!"

It was Charlotte, the Bell's younger daughter. She threw her arms about the robot and squeezed.

Happiness swept over him. "Hello, Charlotte!"

"Are they all here?" she said, stepping back and looking toward the center of the house. "Mum says there are visitors."

"That's right."

"Let's go into the kitchen, then," said Charlotte.

Once there, she hoisted herself onto a worktop, swinging her legs against the cupboard below. Eager looked round for something to offer her. "Would you like a drink, Charlotte?"

"Later," she said. "But I'd love one of those carrots."

Eager handed her the bowl and she took out a raw carrot, which she nibbled as she chatted. She told him about her studies and the funny mistakes she had made. "Just as well I'm still a student doctor," she said.

When his delight at seeing her had died down, Eager remembered that he was looking for Jonquil. He stole glances at the table and worktops while he listened.

"I hate working with animats," Charlotte was saying. "They should have robots like you in hospitals. The animats say all the right things—if the patient looks gloomy they make sympathetic noises, and if the patient makes a joke they smile back— but really they don't have a clue what people are feeling. But you would understand. You'd be much more help." She broke off. "Are you all right, Eager? You look as if you've lost something."

"Do I really?" said Eager delightedly. It always pleased him when his expression was clear to a human. Then he remembered: "Jonquil is a secret," and he tried not to have any expression at all.

"On the other hand," Charlotte continued, "the animats do all the fetching and carrying and they never complain, so they're not entirely useless."

Eager had never met an animat, though he had known other robots in the past.

"You'll be a good doctor," he said.

"Thank you, Eager. I'm trying!"

"When I first met you, I thought you'd never learn anything. But I was wrong." Charlotte burst into peals of laughter. Eager's opinion of her as a baby always amused her. "Now tell me your news," she said, throwing the end of the carrot into the compost box. "Is that sister of yours still bossing you?"

Eager tilted his head. He never considered Allegra bossy, but Charlotte, who'd never met her, had long insisted that this was the case. All he knew was that Allegra would be less than happy to hear that Jonquil had really disappeared this time. What would she say? And how would Eager contact her?

"Eager?" said Charlotte.

"She's working very hard," Eager said hastily. "Some of our experiments are unsuccessful, but others are turning out to be useful."

"Just as I was saying," said Charlotte, jumping down from the worktop. "We could do with robots like you, because you understand what it is to be human." She smiled ruefully. "That's the problem. . . ."

The door opened and Mrs. Bell came in. "Charlotte, you're here!" She hugged her daughter. "I must finish the salad and then we can eat. If you two have finished . . ." She glanced at Eager.

"I'll go and say hello to everyone else," said Charlotte, winking at Eager. He felt overwhelmed by happiness once more.

CHAPTER 13

Finbar stood in a corner of the atrium, a glass of strawberry crush in his hand. He had enjoyed chatting to Mr. and Mrs. Bell and their son, Gavin, who was an engineer and wanted to know all about the Sorbjet. But when Charlotte arrived, Finbar took the opportunity to slip away. He went behind a tall shrub in the corner, with a view of both the courtyard and the house. He found himself looking through the kitchen window at a robot.

It was unlike any robot Finbar had seen before. Its arms and legs seemed to be made of rubber rings. The body was metal and the head a rubber ball. Most startling of all was the robot's behavior. It appeared to be looking for something: opening and shutting cupboards and peeping under surfaces. Or it tapped the appliances and worktops, as if it was blind and depended on touch.

While Finbar watched and tried to find an explanation for the bizarre behavior, he saw his mother come into the kitchen.

Marcia went over to the robot, which had taken the lid off a large jar and was peering inside. The robot turned round. Marcia shook its hand. As Finbar tilted his head, thinking he must have imagined this, Marcia said something else, laid her hand on the robot's shoulder and left the kitchen.

Then Gavin came in. He went straight over to the robot and clasped it by the shoulders. They were standing at an angle to Finbar, but as far as he could tell, Gavin and the robot were having a conversation.

"Mum said to come and talk to you," said a voice behind Finbar that made him jump. He turned round to face Ju.

"Oh!" he said. "I'm fine."

She was eyeing him, as she had when they met outside the house. He felt uncomfortable. "I remember you now," she said. "When we were little we used to wave at each other on the go-between."

"*I* waved," said Finbar. "You scowled, then looked for the camera and tried to poke it."

"Really?" said Ju. There was a pause. She laughed. "You're probably right. What were you looking at in there?"

"Er . . . your grandparents' robot. I've never seen a robot like it before."

The girl frowned. "They don't have a robot. You must mean the one that comes to stay."

Finbar looked at her with curiosity.

"He belongs to friends of theirs. When the friends go away,

they don't like to leave the robot alone so he comes to Gran and Grandpa."

"What's his name?" said Finbar.

"I don't know," said Ju, surprised at the question. "Wait, Edgar, I think."

"He's very un—" Finbar broke off. Ju was staring right past him into the kitchen. Finbar turned round, just in time to see Ju's mother rush up to the robot and kiss it.

For a moment neither watcher said anything. Finbar glanced sideways at Ju: her disbelief mirrored his own. He waited for her to speak first.

"I . . . did you . . . ?"

"I saw it too," said Finbar. "You didn't imagine it. And your mother's not the only one. My mum shook hands with it, and your uncle Gavin held its shoulders."

Ju was staring at Finbar with amazement. "That's strange," she said slowly. "I mean . . . some people get overattached to animats, don't they? And they have to have treatment for it. But no one could ever confuse this robot with a human. . . ."

Finbar nodded. "I'd say they were fond of it, though."

"Is that what people used to do when they had robots? Kiss them?" said Ju. "I don't think that's likely." She turned back to the window as she spoke and her mouth fell open again. Finbar followed her gaze. Fleur was leaning against the table, wiping her eyes with the back of her hand, and the robot was saying something and offering her a paper towel.

"I'm going to fetch the pie!" called Mr. Bell from the atrium. "So everyone to the dining room."

Finbar and Ju exchanged looks and hurried out from behind the plant before anyone could catch them spying.

Finbar held back as the others went into the dining room, hoping to spot the robot. He was lucky—it crossed the hallway ahead of him. "Hello, Edgar."

The robot began to climb the stairs.

"Edgar!" Finbar said, more loudly.

The robot turned his head toward him. "Are you calling me?"

"Maybe this robot isn't so smart," Finbar thought. He was about to move away when the robot said, "You see, my name is Eager."

Finbar had a puzzling urge to apologize for his mistake.

"That's all right," said the robot, smiling. "You must be Finbar. Do you want to go upstairs to lie down?"

"No," said Finbar. Again he felt the need to explain himself. "We had a nap at the hotel, and we've got tablets to help regulate our sleep patterns."

"Professor—" the robot began, and broke off.

"Who?" said Finbar.

The robot said, "I meant to say, people *profess* that the tablets are helpful when they cross different time zones."

"That's right," said Finbar, keeping his eyes on the robot.

"If you'll excuse me . . ." The robot climbed another stair.

Finbar called out, "I saw my mother talking to you in the kitchen."

The robot leant over the banister. "Yes," he said. "Marcia invited me to the theater tomorrow."

Whatever Finbar had expected to hear, this wasn't it. "Have you been to the theater before?" he managed to say.

"With the Bells, a long time ago."

The robot seemed to be waiting for Finbar to say something more. But Finbar was at a loss. "See you tomorrow, then," he said lamely.

The robot smiled. "I shall look forward to it," he said, and continued up the stairs.

CHAPTER 14

Finbar took his place in the dining room.

"I'm so pleased you could all come," Mrs. Bell was saying. "It's a shame your dad isn't here, Ju. Shall we drink a toast to him?"

Everyone raised a glass. "To Sam," they chorused.

"May he soon be home," said Mr. Bell. "It's only a couple more months, isn't it, Fleur?"

Mrs. Bell leant across to Finbar. "Sam is working on the moon," she explained.

"I met a man on the Sorbjet who'd been to the moon," said Finbar.

Before he could say more, Gavin announced loudly, "By the way, Molly is an astrobiologist."

Finbar saw a smile pass between Mrs. Bell and Fleur.

"Astrobiologist, eh?" said Mr. Bell, handing Molly a serving bowl. "So is there life on other planets?"

"There's bound to be," said Molly, helping herself to vegetables.

"That's a sweeping statement," said Fleur.

"To put it in a nutshell," said Molly, "the universe is full of the building blocks of life, and statistically there ought to be other planets that can sustain life. And once life has begun, it tends to get more and more complex. So not only is there life elsewhere, but it could well be intelligent too."

"Really?" said Mr. Bell, giving Molly an admiring look. "And what about life on Mars?" he added.

Molly nodded. "We strongly suspect it was once there. We're just waiting for the robots up there to find more evidence."

"Hang on," said Charlotte. "You're talking about life as we know it. So it needs an atmosphere like Earth to survive. But the Planet-Finder Telescopes have been searching for decades, since before I was born. Forget about Mars . . . they've looked at millions of stars, and there don't seem to be many planets like ours."

"Not *many*," said Molly, laughing. "But how many do you want there to be? It's like looking for a needle in a haystack."

Ju said excitedly, "So if they're like Earth, there's life on them?"

"On one of them, possibly," said Molly. "We'd need to look at countless millions of stars before we found one with life."

"How would you tell?" said Fleur.

"Test their atmospheres to see if they're releasing gases that might come from life processes."

"Like carbon dioxide?" said Fleur.

"Yes. It's very expensive to do, as the planets are so far away. So astronomers have fallen back on the old method," said Molly.

"What's that?" asked Ju.

"Listening," said Molly.

Charlotte helped herself to more vegetables. "Mum, this food is wonderful," she said. There were murmurs of agreement.

"Listening for what?" said Marcia.

"Radio signals," said Molly. "If intelligent life exists, it may well be trying to contact planets like us. We've been listening for signals from outer space for a hundred years."

"Dad's gone to a listening station this weekend," said Ju. "It's on the far side of the moon." Her mother caught her eye and smiled at her.

"And not a peep so far," said Mr. Bell.

Molly shrugged. "That's not quite true," she said. "Though we have nothing definite."

"Go on, tell us!" said Charlotte. "Have aliens ever made contact?"

"It's usually a false alarm," said Molly.

Marcia put down her fork. "How extraordinary, to think there might be planets with advanced civilizations like ours." She tossed her hair over her shoulder.

"I don't know about 'like ours,' " said Molly, smiling. "We're probably backward compared to them. They may have been around for millions of years, if they haven't blown themselves up. Their technology could be far more advanced than ours."

"I can't imagine it . . . ," said Mrs. Bell. "What do advanced civilizations do all day? Lie around eating grapes?"

"Is that what you'd do, Mum?" teased Gavin.

Ju had an image of her grandmother being fed grapes by a seven-armed alien. She choked with laughter. "I'm OK," she spluttered as Charlotte thumped her on the back.

"If we were more advanced," Gavin was saying, "we could harness the physical laws of the universe even more than we do now. . . . We could fly and send messages telepathically. We could create matter out of thin air!"

"Abracadabra! Turn this fish pie into gold!" cried Ju, tapping her plate with the end of her knife. Everyone laughed as she frowned in mock disappointment. "Looks like we've a long way to go."

"Is something wrong with the fish pie?" asked her mum.

"It's delicious," said Ju. "Did you make it, Gran?"

"With a little help from Eager," said Mrs. Bell.

There was a lull in the conversation. The pie was offered a second time. Finbar was pleased when Marcia declined and Mrs. Bell insisted he have an extra-large helping. He gave his mother a shrug, to say "Well, one of us has to show appreciation."

"If you think they exist, Molly, why haven't alien civilizations visited us?" said Mr. Bell. "Surely they'd have got here by now."

"It's possible that they have," said Molly.

There was a mixture of laughter and protest from around the table.

"No, really!" she said. "People used to laugh at the idea twenty years ago, but some scientists think it might have happened, given the immense age of the universe. We're a young planet. Aliens might have come millions of years ago, before there was intelligent life. They could still be watching us."

"But the stars you've been talking about are oodles of light-years away," said Charlotte. "Since you can't travel faster than the speed of light, it would take oodles and oodles of years to get here."

"Oodles, eh?" said Gavin. "That must be a scientific term. Is it longer or shorter than a noodle?"

Charlotte glared affectionately at her brother.

"Charlotte's right," said Molly solemnly. "It could take zillions of oodles of years to get here."

"What if there's a habitable star quite close to Earth?" said Finbar. "How far away would that be?"

"It would still be hundreds or thousands of years away," said Molly. "They'd have to send colonies into space to breed for centuries and centuries until it was time to land here."

"Unless they sent robots," said Charlotte.

"Couldn't an advanced civilization achieve the speed of light or beyond? And get to us more quickly?" said Gavin.

"In theory," said Molly, "but it would take a massive amount of energy. They may not think it worthwhile. That's why radio signals are the best form of contact."

"Why exactly?" said Finbar.

"Because they're cheaper, and you can send signals round the clock. And the universe is full of radio waves, so it's an obvious technology for all intelligent life to know about. But imagine staring into space—where do you send your message? Which direction? What frequency?" The door opened and Eager came into the dining room.

"Shall I clear the plates, Mrs. Bell?" he asked.

"Yes, please," she said.

Molly leant across the table toward Mrs. Bell. "What an interesting robot," she said.

"He is," said Mrs. Bell. "He belongs to friends of ours. We have him to stay when they go away."

Molly said excitedly, "Wouldn't it be fascinating if we discovered that extraterrestrials were robots? I don't just mean intelligent machines, like this one. What if they have humanlike consciousness . . . ?"

The conversations around the table petered into silence. Finbar noticed Mrs. Bell shaking her head warningly at her husband. And from the corner of his eye he saw his mother smile knowingly at Gavin. He was puzzled.

"Eager," said Molly as the robot took her plate, "what's the name of the family you belong to?"

Eager was taken aback. He had never expected to be asked this question. He held the plate in midair as he searched his memory for a likely name. Looking across at Mrs. Bell, he saw from the frown on her face that she too was at a loss.

"Jones," he said.

Molly erupted into laughter. "Jones!" she spluttered.

"Not *the* Jones family, I hope," said Ju. "I'd go mad if I lived with the Jones family!"

"So would I," agreed Molly. "I couldn't bear all that melodrama."

Charlotte said, "It's a good thing Eager *doesn't* live with Lori. She can't even make herself a cup of tea without having an accident."

Eager had a conviction that he had said the wrong thing. He looked helplessly at Mrs. Bell.

"It's a common name," Gavin said. "But . . . er, Fred Jones and . . ."

"Paula," said his mother.

"Yes, Paula—they're a nice quiet couple, aren't they, Mum? Would you bring in the puddings, Eager? . . . Eager?"

The robot was staring into the middle distance.

"I'll get them," said Charlotte, leaping up.

"I'll help," said Fleur.

"They're on the kitchen table," said their mother.

Eager turned on his heels and followed them out of the room.

CHAPTER 15

Eager went straight upstairs, determined to find his nephew this time. He strode into the gobetween room. "Jonquil!" No response. He went from room to room, throwing open cupboards and patting the tops of beds. It was rare that Eager felt exasperated, and he stopped to experience the emotion. He resumed his search with fierce concentration.

After he'd gone through every room in the house, with the exception of the dining room, where everyone was still eating, he stood in the kitchen and pondered Jonquil's disappearance. His nephew was curious and had never before left the compound where he lived; maybe he'd gone outside to explore. Eager hastened toward the front door. The dining room door was open and he could hear people talking.

"Apple tart?" said Mrs. Bell.

And then Gavin's voice, "No, thanks, I'll have some of this meringue."

Eager had not made a meringue. Nor had he noticed one in the kitchen. He doubled back and peered into the room. Mrs.

Bell, who was nearest the door, wore a mystified expression. Gavin stood with a knife in his hand, poised to cut into a squashed white confection on the table.

Eager extended the rubber rings of his arm and snatched up the plate just as Gavin brought the knife down. The blade struck the table, rattling the dishes and glassware. Gavin gave Eager a startled look.

"It isn't cooked." Eager drew the plate to his chest.

"Looks perfect to me," protested Gavin. "I like a gooey center."

Eager hoped Jonquil had not overheard this description. "It isn't cooked," he repeated.

"I'd advise against eating raw egg white," said Fleur.

Gavin frowned. "Is something wrong with the oven, Mum?"

"I think there might be," Mrs. Bell said. "It was the wrong temperature this morning."

"Have some apple tart instead," said Charlotte.

"Yes, Doctor," said Gavin good-humoredly. "So long as I can have plenty of cream with it."

Meanwhile, Eager had hurried to the kitchen with the meringue-Jonquil. The door opened and Molly came in. Eager jumped round to face her, the plate still in his hand.

"We'd better throw that away," she said.

"Yes," said Eager without moving. He put down the plate casually, as if it held no importance for him, and smiled at Molly. After a pause she smiled back and left the kitchen.

Eager seized the plate. "Jonquil! Can you hear me?" he cried.

"You should have rested upstairs. You haven't recovered your energy yet!"

The door opened again and Marcia appeared. Eager couldn't help glaring at her, although he wished he hadn't. Luckily Marcia didn't seem to notice.

"We're leaving now, Eager. Don't forget the theater tomorrow. I'll send a pod to collect you. Fleur and Ju are coming as well. Isn't that wonderful!"

CHAPTER 16

It was midnight before Jonquil was fully recovered. While Mr. and Mrs. Bell slept, Eager remonstrated with his nephew in the gobetween room. "If I hadn't rescued you, Gavin would have sliced you in two," he said.

"I came downstairs to see the visitors. Then I felt weak . . . ," said Jonquil. He was paper-shaped, one edge firmly on the floor, the rest of him swaying slightly as he spoke.

"And somehow you ended up on a plate in the dining room," said Eager. "And another thing—"

"You sound like Mr. Jones, when he discovers that Lori has been surfing at night."

"That's what I want to talk about," said Eager.

"Surfing?" said Jonquil.

"The Jones family. They are not a real family at all. It's a story on the gobetween. It's called a soap opera. Mrs. Bell explained it to me while we were tidying up this evening. The Joneses aren't even real people anymore, since the actors couldn't work long enough hours. Now the characters are computer simulations."

Jonquil greeted the news with silence.

"So we must tell Allegra to expect you tomorrow night," said Eager. "I'm going to the theater." He had a twinge of expectation as he said this. "I asked Mr. and Mrs. Bell and they think it's all right for me to go."

"Theater?" said Jonquil. "What's that?"

Eager had to think for a moment. "It's like a soap opera. People pretend to be other people, and other people, the audience, go to watch what happens to them."

"What happens to who?" said Jonquil.

"The people the first people are pretending to be."

"Why?" said Jonquil.

Eager said, "Why what?"

Jonquil became a ball and rolled away. "Never mind. I'll see for myself."

"No you won't," said Eager. "I shall send you home first."

Jonquil flew onto his shoulder. "I can't go yet! I haven't seen anything of life!"

"Because you're too busy avoiding destruction!" Eager said. "We must call Allegra now. Will you connect the gobetween to her?"

His nephew jumped into a starburst, glowing golden. "No, I won't," he said. He landed on the carpet, flattened himself and slipped under the door.

By the time the door had opened to let Eager out, Jonquil was nowhere to be seen. The robot tilted his head. He needed to think quickly. "Jonquil," he said, "if you can hear me, I have a suggestion. You can come to the theater, if you talk to Allegra. We can ask her what she thinks we should do." He added, "She needs to know that you're safe."

A piece of the ceiling above Eager fell toward him. Automatically he stepped backward, then—oh! Jonquil.

"All right, Uncle Eager. I'll talk to Mother. And you must take me to the theater."

They went back into the gobetween room, and Eager showed his nephew the control box. "I'm already inside," said Jonquil.

Instantly, Allegra's face appeared on the screen. She nodded with pleasure as she saw Jonquil.

Jonquil lost his bravado. "Mother," he said faintly. Eager wondered—was his nephew feeling the aftermath of his experiences? Perhaps he had a fear mechanism after all.

But Jonquil quickly recovered. "I'm having a wonderful time," he said, radiating starbursts.

A man with unruly white hair appeared behind Allegra. "Professor Ogden!" cried Eager as the man stepped forward. The appearance of the familiar face caused him a moment's confusion.

"Hello, Eager," said the professor. "And hello, Jonquil. I hear you stowed away." His tone was stern. Eager noticed the twinkle in his eye, but Jonquil could not discern such details.

In a flash, he crossed the room and disappeared under the door.

Professor Ogden chuckled. "Are you happy to be back with the Bells, Eager?"

Eager stopped to think. He had been too busy chasing after Jonquil to consider whether he was enjoying himself. Then he remembered his pleasure at seeing the Bells and their children again. "Yes, I am," he said. "And Marcia is here too."

"Good heavens, Marcia!" said Professor Ogden. "I was reminded of her the other day, for some reason."

"She's invited me to the theater tomorrow night. Is it all right to go, Professor?"

The professor reflected. "I don't see why not, so long as you don't draw attention to yourself. Of course, people will notice you, but they'll probably assume you're a robot of the old school."

Eager said hastily, "Jonquil is coming too. I was thinking I should send him home afterward."

"Tomorrow night, you mean?" The professor stared at the floor. "It would be better if he stayed with you," he said at last.

Eager thought about the word "better." Better for him, or for Jonquil, or for Professor Ogden, or for Allegra? And better than what?

The professor said, "I can't explain now, but it's best to avoid unnecessary comings and goings at present. And we shouldn't talk for long on the gobetween, even though Jonquil has connected us."

This took a moment to sink in. "Professor Ogden, when I return at the end of the week, will you still be there?"

The pause before the professor replied was longer than expected. "I very much hope so, Eager," he said.

CHAPTER 17

Her mother liked to lie in at the weekend, but Ju never managed that. She woke at first light and lay there, deciphering the still fuzzy outlines of the objects in the room.

Then she remembered two things. One: her father would be out of contact all weekend. Two: she was going to the theater with Marcia and Finbar.

The second thought led to other recollections—meeting Finbar; hiding behind the shrub with him and watching the robot; and the way they had caught each other's eye during supper, at strange moments in the conversation.

She slipped out of bed and padded in bare feet to the kitchen. She found a fruit bun, which she sliced in half and put in the toaster. "Toaster, is it safe to eat?"

"I detect no hazardous organisms," said the toaster.

"Lightly toasted, then," said Ju.

The green light by the door flashed. "The homechef has devised the perfect breakfast for you," said the gobetween, "with particular attention to your calcium requirement."

"Whatever it is, I bet it's green," said Ju. She piled butter and strawberry jam onto the bun. "I'll just eat this first. . . ."

She put the bun on a saucer and went out to the terrace. Birdsong greeted her as she sat down at the table. This was her favorite time of day, before the hurry and bustle began. Even the delivery pods overhead appeared to fly at a more leisurely pace than normal.

While she ate, she admired the flowers in the tubs. She hoped they would stay in bloom until her dad's return. Thinking of her dad, Ju felt restless. She went back into the living area and sat cross-legged on the floor, facing the gobetween screen.

"I'm ready for a story, Gobey. But keep any sound effects down. I don't want to wake Mum." Ju loved telling stories. Not with words, which she found cumbersome and flat, but with pictures. She started with the image—the picture in her mind—and made it physical. She added more images, stirred these ingredients with her imagination and waited to see what was created. Every story was an experiment.

"Gobey," she began, "find me a girl. My age, but prettier. No, wait! Why are heroines always pretty? Make her wild-looking."

A girl appeared on the screen, holding a spear. She was heavily built, with a large jaw and forehead. Her hair was matted, her cheeks mud-stained. She was wrapped in a skin, knotted at one shoulder. Something must have caught her eye, for she raised the spear menacingly and bared her teeth.

"Not that kind of wild!" said Ju. "I meant brave and daring, not savage."

"Aren't hunters brave and daring?" said the gobetween.

"Of course they're brave," said Ju. "That doesn't make them interesting. This girl only cares about killing her next meal. I'm thinking of someone who's daring because she does things differently."

"If you meant unconventional, you should have said so," said the gobetween. Yet the thought had come to Ju: "I'm the storyteller—it's my job to make her interesting." What if the girl found an animal that she did not want to kill; instead she grew fond of it? How would that affect her? What would the rest of the tribe do?

"I'll search for another girl," said the gobetween.

"No, I'll keep her. Now find me an animal—a really cute one."

It took a long time for the gobetween to produce something that pleased Ju. A succession of kittens, foals, puppies, deer and lambs skittered, gamboled and trotted across the screen. A newborn giraffe struggled to rise on long spindly legs, a kangaroo peered blindly from its mother's pouch and a seal cub rolled fetchingly onto its back. Ju rejected them all.

"It has to be something the girl has never seen before."

"An elephant?"

"No," said Ju firmly. A trunk that had edged its way onto the screen disappeared.

"I have it." The gobetween sounded triumphant. "I've placed it in the tree behind the girl."

"It's my story," said Ju, but she was intrigued. She watched as the huntress, smelling that night's dinner, turned warily on her heels. Crouching low, she approached the tree in a few silent paces. She waited for a second before raising the arm with the spear. Ju felt a lump in her throat.

"Don't let her kill it," she breathed. "She makes friends with it. . . ."

The tree rustled. Between the leaves a smooth black nugget appeared, followed by a triangular face and the hairiest ears Ju had ever seen. Long fingers parted the branches, revealing a plump body covered in fur. It was a koala.

There came a point in her storytelling when Ju was so engrossed that she no longer needed to speak. By then the gobetween could read her brain patterns and knew her thoughts before she voiced them.

"The girl wants to kill him, but she mustn't succeed. The koala does something to stop her."

Already the huntress was raising her spear. The koala let go of the branches and keeled over backward. The foliage gave way with a loud whoosh, as if buffeted by a furious wind. Then silence.

The girl looked around and sniffed the air before peering into the tree. The gobetween showed her close up. Ju could see the uneven splodges of mud on her face, the tangled hair, the fear and determination in her brown eyes. A meter or so below lay the koala, suspended on a lattice of branches and leaves. His eyes were shut, his body rigid.

"Not dead," thought Ju. But he would be soon. The huntress drew back her spear, ready to plunge it into the creature's soft belly.

The koala's eyes opened and he sat up. A glance at the spearhead, poised to end his life, and he shut his eyes, throwing himself backward again.

The huntress laughed, and so did Ju. Whatever had gone on in the koala's head, he was lucky to have a comic's sense of timing. The huntress laughed so much that she lowered the spear, though she was too thoroughly trained to drop it altogether.

Laughing interrupted the flow of Ju's thoughts. "How is he going to get out of there?" she said aloud. "He can't stay like that forever."

Her first idea was to have the animal wave his arms in the air, like a baby demanding to be lifted from his cot. But the koala, she decided, was too cheeky and knowing for that. Instead, she imagined him opening his eyes and meeting the girl's curious gaze with an impudent stare.

The tension between them was so strong that it was an effort for Ju to hold it in her mind. For the huntress was battling with herself. She needed to kill to survive, yet the longer she looked at the animal, the less funny and the more courageous he appeared.

At last Ju had her come to a decision. The girl swiveled the spear between her finger and thumb so that the blade pointed behind her, and lowered the end toward the koala. As soon as he was able, he sprang onto the shaft, wrapping his long limbs around it. He was surprisingly heavy. The girl had to brace herself as she took his weight.

The koala jumped from the spear and into the girl's arms. Far from clinging to her gratefully, he sat up like a child emperor, twisting his head round as if to indicate the direction he wanted to go in.

"She's stuck with him now," said Ju. "I see! They're a team. The girl protects him and he helps her hunt."

She was delighted with her creations. There were lots of stories here. The huntress was not so predictable after all, and the koala was a fun pet—well, hardly a pet, more of a companion.

"That's it for today, Gobey," Ju said.

The koala jumped down from the girl's arms and loped on all fours toward Ju, like an actor relaxing after a day's filming.

"Do you like me?" he said, causing her to jump.

The voice, though not particularly deep, had a hint of a growl in it. She had not thought of making him speak, for she wanted the story to be realistic. Irritably, she said, "Gobey, why are you making him talk?"

Unusually, the gobetween did not reply.

"Do you like me?" repeated the animal.

"What do you want?" said Ju. "I'm not imagining you now, so why are you still here?"

"You do like me, don't you?" he said, undeterred.

"Yes, I like you. I'm going to make up stories about you. But why are you talking to me?" said Ju.

"Would you like me to be with you?"

Ju became exasperated. "You can't be with me. The gobetween found you, but you don't exist outside the screen."

The koala rubbed his shiny nose with a forefinger as if to polish it further. "I could," he persisted. He waved toward the huntress, who was standing behind him, expressionless. "You could carry me around like she does. You could tell me things, and I could help you."

"Don't be ridiculous. We could appear to be together on the screen, but we can't be physically. Don't you understand how the gobetween works?"

Ju realized what a stupid question this was. As if a koala could understand how a universal communication system worked!

"Just go away," she said. "I mean it."

The koala gave her a doleful look and loped back to the huntress. They walked out of sight together.

"Gobey! What's going on?" said Ju. "Why did you bring the koala back?"

"I didn't," said the deep voice. "He came of his own volition."

"His own what?"

"Will," said the gobetween. "I had no control over him."

"But you found him in the first place. How did you do that?"

"The usual way," said the gobetween. "Some characters I find for you from other people's stories. Or I might find a picture that suits your requirements. Some are real people—"

Ju interrupted. "Is that legal?"

"It happens all the time. I regret that I do not know the law on this matter. I could find out. . . ."

It struck her that someone, somewhere, might be thinking up a story in which she was one of the principal characters. She was not sure how she felt about that.

The gobetween continued, "This koala appears to be an animat. He's for sale. I am sorry that I was unable to discover this at the time. I have to scan zillions of bits of information—it happens in a picosecond and I can't check where all the information is coming from, you understand."

Ju did understand. She stood up. "I'm not blaming you. But I don't want him talking in my stories, agreed?"

"Very well."

CHAPTER 18

Finbar had a busy morning. He joined his mother at a breakfast meeting with a gallery owner who wanted to display her paintings. After they had eaten, Marcia was still talking and the gallery owner, a young man with floppy hair, was hanging on to her every word.

Finbar excused himself and went to find the hotel gobeyhall. It was in the basement, and the booking clerk told him that a liveball game was about to begin. He went into the room, where six other people of mixed ages were standing in the half-light.

The screen that surrounded them on four sides came to life, revealing a stadium with a cheering crowd. Daylight shone. A muscular figure strode onto the pitch. "I'm Todd Bryant," he told the waiting players, though he had no need to introduce himself. Anyone interested in liveball would have recognized him as a well-known player.

"What level are you all?" he said.

There was a murmured discussion. Everyone agreed that they

97

would prefer a level just above easy. "OK. You're all playing against my team. Let's go," said Todd. He raised his hand and his teammates ran onto the pitch.

A ball appeared on the screen, ducking and swooping as the players reached for it. The people in the gobeyhall kept their eyes on the ball, but no one was prepared to chase it at first.

Then the ball flew straight into their midst; a boy leapt for it, missed and tried again. Another boy dived at it, and it veered away. The game had begun.

Finbar threw himself into the chase, enjoying the exercise. For a long time Todd's team, though playing far below their ability, scored repeatedly. Eventually, Finbar's team found a strategy to corner the ball. They lost the game, but by a respectable margin. Finbar's one disappointment was that he could not touch a real liveball but only chase its shadow.

"Good play," said Todd before he faded from the screen.

After lunch, Finbar's mother had booked a massage. He said he would go for a walk. One of the things Finbar liked about his parents was that they did not fuss. As long as there was no apparent danger, they didn't scare themselves imagining what might happen if he went off on his own.

As he walked past shops, weaving through the crowds, he saw that the window displays were multiple miniworlds—jungle, tundra, outer space, sunlit gardens. . . . It became a game to discover what the store was actually selling.

Finbar craned his neck to see the billscreens above. They too created their own three-dimensional universe. He gaped at a tropical rain forest, a cat and an eardrum, all blown up to immense size, and with sound effects. A man was standing in front of one, listening to a grand piano playing jazz. A voice said, "Mr. Klein, when did you last update your sound system? Don't tell me, I know. . . ."

Finbar shook his head. He wasn't used to cities. They were too hectic, too dazzling and intrusive. He turned to walk back to the hotel.

"Hey, you!"

Finbar spun round to discover that the speaker was an animat demonstrating dance steps to a group of children. Finbar turned the corner and could see the hotel at the end of the street.

"Hi there, Finbar."

Startled, he looked round for the speaker. A young man in a dark suit smiled at him from a solitary billscreen.

"How do you know my name?"

"Your jinn, of course." The man raised an eyebrow. "It also tells me that you passed through immigration yesterday, so you must be new in town."

Finbar was reminded of very old movies that he had seen, and wanted to laugh. "So what if I am?" he said, adopting a similar mocking tone.

The man grinned. "There must be things you need. What do you like to do? Gobeyhalls? Racetracks? Liveball games? I can get you tickets for them all, and arrange for pods to take you there. Want to make new friends? I can—"

"No, I don't want any of it. At least, not through you." Finbar walked on, quickening his step.

"Hey! You don't know what you're missing! Let me show you some of . . ."

Finbar broke into a run.

CHAPTER 19

Finbar's mother lay on her bed, reading from her new lexiscreen. He sat down. "A billscreen spoke to me, just outside the hotel. I mean, called me by name," he said indignantly.

"Billscreens can pick up your identity from your jinn."

"It knew that I'd arrived here yesterday. . . ."

"Don't worry. Your bank account, shoe size and secret messages are quite safe. A billscreen can only pick up basic information that you might pass on to anyone who asks."

"But it didn't ask," said Finbar. "That's the point."

"You need to wear a device that blocks out the signals from your jinn. It's a little tab that sits inside your sleeve," said Marcia. She smiled knowingly at him. "Why don't you have some put into your new clothes? Call Whittaker and Co and ask."

He stared at her. "What new—?"

She held up a hand to silence him. "I know, I've said too much. You want to surprise me. It's a lovely thing to do, and I'm looking forward to seeing you wear them to the theater. Now, I don't know about you, but I need a nap before then."

Finbar went to his own room, where he sat on the edge of the bed, frowning. "New clothes," he said wonderingly. What was she talking about?

Finbar wasn't interested in his appearance, to Marcia's great disappointment. He bought his own clothes, out of his monthly allowance, nothing fashionable, and wore them until they were threadbare.

One day his mother had said to him, "I don't want you to think you can't afford good clothes, so I'm giving you access to my own account. Buy whatever you like and charge it to me."

Now Finbar pulled back his sleeve. "Jinn, show me my monthly account."

Rows of numbers scrolled down the screen. Right. No clothes that month. He had to take a deep breath before going on.

"Now show me my mother's account."

It was there: an entry with today's date—"Whittaker and Co"—followed by a figure that made Finbar gasp. Whittaker and Co: that was the store with the waterfall. How on earth could he have bought clothes there?

Finbar sat staring into space. Someone had apparently bought clothes. Was it his mother? Was she pretending to know nothing about them in the hope that he would feel so guilty that he would wear them? He looked at the door, half-expecting her to come in, an evening suit over her arm. No, this was too devious, even for his mother.

He imagined breaking the news to her: "Mum, I know you're

looking forward to seeing them, but the bad news is I haven't bought any clothes. The worse news is someone else has."

Where were the clothes? The answer came to him in a flash. With the thief, of course. "Jinn," Finbar said, "get me Whittaker and Co."

While he waited to be connected, he closed the curtains so that he would be seen in shadow. A hearty-looking man appeared on the screen. It was hard to tell whether he was human or animat.

"Good afternoon, Mr. Khan. How can I help you?"

"Er . . . we haven't met, have we?" said Finbar.

"I didn't have that pleasure today, sir," said the man. "I don't work in the young men's department." He went on, "We've finished the alterations. Your clothes are all ready."

"*My* clothes," repeated Finbar.

"That's right, sir."

Finbar's mind was racing. "Er . . . I've forgotten what address I gave you," he said. "I'm a bit jet-lagged, and . . . I've changed hotels since I arrived."

"You said you might, sir. So you were going to send a pod to collect the clothes, rather than have them delivered. We were expecting it any moment."

The thief was clever, but it seemed that Finbar was a step ahead!

"Well, I've changed my mind," said Finbar. "I'd like you to deliver them to the Hotel Regency."

"Very well, sir."

"In case there's a mix-up and a pod still arrives, just send it away, please."

"Of course, sir."

Finbar threw himself onto the bed. What a relief! At least the clothes would soon be in his possession. As he relaxed, sleep came.

Forty-five minutes later he sat up, blinking. There was a knock at the door. An animat stood there, holding a slim white box with WHITTAKER AND CO emblazoned on it in gold letters.

"Mr. Khan?"

"That's me." Panic seized him as he considered that the animat would require proof of his identity but his retinogram wouldn't match the person who had ordered the clothes. Taking a cue from his mother, he decided that boldness was the best defense.

"Do you want to take a retinogram?" he said cheerfully.

"Oh, no," said the animat. "If I could just scan your jinn . . ."

Finbar held out his wrist and the animat waved his hand above it and handed Finbar the box. It felt heavy. "Goodbye, sir. Enjoy your purchase."

"Not for long," thought Finbar as he closed the door. The very next day he would take the clothes back. He removed the lid. A sea of tissue paper hid the contents.

"Thank you for shopping at Whittaker and Co," said a cultivated voice. "We hope you enjoy your purchase. Please note

that if you have bought handmade clothes and had them finished to your specifications, there is no refund."

There was a peal of music. A list of cleaning instructions followed, but Finbar was staring at the box in shock. Of course,
the clothes had been altered. He could not take them back.
Nor could he wear them, even if he wanted to. They would be
men's clothes, to fit the thief. Gingerly, he pulled away the last
of the tissue paper.

CHAPTER 28

It was a perfect summer evening when Ju and Fleur set out for the theater. Normally quiet streets were full of people strolling, or eating at outdoor cafés. Ju would have liked to linger, but they were late and her mother marched her along.

The theater had recently been built in the heart of the city, at the end of a tree-lined avenue. It was big and round, divided into equal segments like a giant orange. Most people called it the Big Orange.

On a billscreen above the entrance, life-size figures in doublet and hose were sword-fighting. Instinctively, Ju ducked as she hurried into the foyer. It took a moment to realize that she was standing in one of the segments: it curved around her like an upended boat.

"I didn't read the name of the play," she wailed. "I still don't know what it's about."

"Too late," said Fleur.

Marcia, Finbar and Eager sat waiting for them. Ju laughed,

for the robot was reading a lexiscreen. "Look, Mum," she said. "Marcia wasn't joking, she's brought Edgar."

Her mother looked crossly at her. "Eager," she said.

"No need to rush," Marcia called.

Eager looked up. "Hello, Fleur. I'm just reading about the play, since I'm unfamiliar with the sixteenth century."

"You're not the only one," thought Ju. She said, "Can I have a look?"

"Certainly," said the robot. As he handed over the lexiscreen, the adults stood up to go and he followed them.

Finbar sat as if reluctant to move. Ju overheard Marcia whisper to Fleur, "New clothes. Not quite what I would have chosen, but I'm delighted he's showing an interest at last."

The women moved off, leaving Ju staring at Finbar. He was wearing a suit of sorts in a glittery turquoise fabric. When he stood up, Ju saw that the jacket sleeves touched his knuckles, while the trousers collected in folds at his ankles.

There was a silence.

"What possessed you?" said Ju.

Absurdly, Finbar wanted to laugh. There wasn't a trace of concern in Ju's voice. Yet to hear someone acknowledge that these clothes were not normal for him—that they were a ghastly, ridiculous mistake—was a huge relief. "They're nothing to do with me!" he said.

Now Ju was sympathetic. "Did your mum choose them, really?" she said.

"I wish she had," groaned Finbar, pulling at his sleeve. "Her taste couldn't be worse than this."

An animat came over to them. "Excuse me, sir, madam— *Romeo and Juliet* is about to begin."

Finbar came to his senses. He had only just met Ju and he'd been on the verge of telling her about the theft. What possessed him, indeed?

※ ※ ※ ※ ※

Eager's anxiety about the evening began to lift. The audience was too busy admiring the building to notice him, and Jonquil was safely disguised across his shoulders. Ever since they'd left the Bells' house, his nephew had been unusually quiet. Seeing Professor Ogden on the gobetween appeared to have calmed him down.

Eager followed Marcia into the auditorium and lost his balance. The world was shifting around him. He stood still and tried to make sense of what was happening.

"What's the matter, Uncle Eager?" said Jonquil's voice.

Eager realized that the building itself was moving, unfurling as if an unseen hand was opening the orange. The segments tilted slowly backward, leaving the auditorium open to the sky. The people inside stood around, craning to watch.

Within each segment were three tiers of seating, reached by a spiral staircase. In a final movement, the seats tipped forward to be level with the ground. There was a round of applause.

"Is anything happening?" said Jonquil.

"Ladies and gentlemen," came an announcement, "you may now take your seats for tonight's performance of *Romeo and Juliet*. Please ensure that your jinns and other devices are in silent mode."

"I have to find my seat," said Eager.

Yet nobody sat down. Everyone was milling around. There was the sound of music—strings and a wind instrument—and cries of "Strawberries! Cherries ripe!"

"Aieee! So noisy!" said Jonquil.

Eager tried to find Marcia and Fleur, but a woman carrying a large basket blocked his way. She was warmly dressed for the time of year, in a long skirt and full-length sleeves and with a small cap on her head. "What can I offer ye? Meat pie? French walnuts?" she said with a smile.

"No, thank you," said Eager. "I don't eat."

"You'll be wanting an ale, then?"

"A nail?" said Eager, glancing down to check that he was in one piece. "I'm not that sort of robot."

"Not that sort! Why"—the woman nudged him as she spoke—"there's no harm in a healthy thirst, especially for a lusty young gentleman like you."

"Go and find another customer," said a firm voice behind Eager. It was Finbar. The woman bent at the knees and bobbed up again before walking away.

Eager turned round to thank the boy.

Finbar said, "You must be stern and speak clearly, otherwise animats will keep on offering their services. That's what they're programmed to do."

"I see," said Eager. He noticed more women in long skirts, carrying trays. People were queuing to buy food from them.

Through the crowds appeared the musicians, all men. They too wore curious clothes—balloonlike shorts over colored leggings, and shirts with voluminous striped sleeves.

"Come on, Ju's waving at us," said Finbar, pointing ahead. "She went to find Mum and Fleur."

"Isn't it wonderful!" said Marcia as they approached. "So Elizabethan."

"But without the smells, the gambling, the drunken brawls . . . ," said Fleur.

As the audience shuffled along the rows of seats, the food sellers and musicians headed for a raised platform that stretched across three segments of the building. It was covered by a wide canopy.

Eager found himself sitting between Ju and Marcia. He shifted in his seat to get the best view.

"Hey, robot, remove your headgear!" a voice called. "I can't see the stage."

Eager put his hand to his head and felt the wiry tangle of Jonquil. "Get down," he said in his thoughts.

"My sight line is blocked. I can't see," said Jonquil.

"Neither can the man behind," thought Eager. "Try the seat in front."

Jonquil climbed up the back of the seat, turning as red as the fabric as he went. He huddled on the top left corner.

"Two households both alike in dignity, in fair Verona where we lay our scene . . . ," a woman was saying. As she continued, Eager caught the words "death," "love," and "rage."

"Just like the Jones family," said Jonquil excitedly.

". . . in this the two hours' traffic of our stage," said the woman.

"Two hours," Ju grumbled, "two long hours."

Some men came onto the stage. Eager could tell that they were playing, but the next minute they had quarreled with other men, and the two factions were slashing at each other with swords. People came and went. A man with a thunderous voice, and wearing a fur-trimmed hat, put a stop to the fighting.

"What's happening?" said Jonquil.

Eager was glad that he had read the lexiscreen. "Two families quarrel all the time. Their servants were just fighting and the prince stopped them—"

"Just like Mr. Jones and his neighbors."

A handsome young man appeared. He must be Romeo. He talked a lot about love and looked very gloomy.

The scene changed to a house where the girl, Juliet, lived. Her nurse summoned her to her mother, who told Juliet that she was going to be married. Ju gasped and whispered to Finbar, "She's only thirteen!"

At first Ju had struggled to understand a language that sounded both familiar and alien. But by the time Juliet met Romeo, Ju had forgotten about the rows of seats separating her from the stage. She saw only the splendor of a ballroom, lit by burning torches, where danger and love danced together.

She believed in the lovers' whispered promises; she believed in the moonlight shining on them; and while she did not understand all their jokes as Romeo's friends searched for him, she believed in their high spirits.

She knew exactly how Juliet was feeling the next day when the nurse was late in bringing news from Romeo: ". . . from nine till twelve is three long hours, yet she is not come. . . ."

Ju felt a foreboding of death as the lovers married in secret. She was right. Juliet's cousin killed Romeo's mad, talkative friend, and Romeo, in fury, killed the cousin.

The lights came up for the interval and Ju saw that the sky had become dark without her noticing.

"Are you enjoying it?" said Marcia's voice.

Ju turned to respond, but Marcia had been addressing Eager.

"Very much, thank you," said the robot. "It's surprising: none of it is real, but I felt fearful, happy, sad and worried, as if everything was really happening."

The robot froze, as if his system had stalled.

"Eager, are you all right?" said Marcia.

"Yes, thank you," he said, his eyes fixed on the back of the seat in front of him.

"We're going for a drink," said Fleur, leaning across Marcia to speak to him. "We'll see you later."

Eager waited until everyone had gone before saying in a low voice, "Jonquil, where are you? Jonquil?"

The woman sitting in front of Eager stood up, leaving behind the lower part of her long dark hair across the top of her seat. Eager jumped at the sight and just stopped himself from calling out to the woman. The remainder of her hair began to turn red. A second later, it fell weightlessly onto Eager's lap.

The red fibers became straw-colored.

"Do we go home now?" said Jonquil.

"No," said Eager. "The audience is having a rest."

"I knew there was going to be an accident after the boy kissed the girl," said Jonquil. "I was surprised she didn't fall off the balcony. Perhaps she'll get run over in a minute."

"There have been a lot of deaths," Eager said.

"That happens in the Jones family too," said Jonquil. "They use laser guns. Those silver sticks are more exciting."

Instantly, he was a long thin blade, slashing and stabbing the air.

"Get down!" cried Eager. The people still in the auditorium looked round.

The sword made a flourish, then dissolved itself into a golden ball. Jonquil drifted back to Eager's lap until the end of the interval.

CHAPTER 21

The second half of the play was full of doom, as Ju had predicted. Romeo was banished from Verona for killing Juliet's cousin. Juliet's father was going to force her to marry another man, called Paris. To avoid marrying him, Juliet drank a sleeping potion that made her appear dead. A message was sent to Romeo in hiding, but he did not receive it.

Believing that Juliet had indeed died, he went to her tomb to kill himself. Paris, bringing flowers to the grave, tried to stop him entering it. Romeo and Paris fought. Ju wasn't sentimental, but this play had too many deaths and not enough love for her. She fidgeted. Finbar whispered, "It gets worse."

"How worse?" she hissed.

"Romeo kills himself just before Juliet wakes up. She sees him dead and kills herself too."

"Great," said Ju.

On the stage, Paris dropped his sword and fell to the ground.

"O, I am slain," he cried.

Eager understood this to mean killed, and felt pity. Paris was a nice man, and no one had explained to him that Juliet loved someone else.

". . . lay me with Juliet," he begged as he died.

Eager was pleased when Romeo pulled open the door to the tomb and dragged Paris inside. The stage revolved to show Juliet, lying on a stone tomb.

"She's going to wake up soon, isn't she?" said Jonquil. "The potion that the man gave her was to make her sleep, wasn't it?"

A moment later he cried, "Why doesn't the boy sit down and wait for her to wake up?" Eager was too busy watching Romeo to notice.

There was a sound of twigs hitting the floor.

Jonquil's fibers were choked with fine dust from beneath the seats. He flew up and hopped onto Marcia's lap, and from there to Fleur and the next person, until he reached the end of the row. Under cover of darkness, he flew down the center aisle, gathering speed that boosted him onto the stage. He found himself on a richly colored rug. Juliet was lying next to him, her arms folded across her body, her eyes closed. Her long hair streamed beside her on the pillow.

Ju felt a tightening across her chest. If only Romeo had received the friar's message! Now he believed that Juliet was really dead, and he was going to kill himself. It was such a waste.

"Here, here will I remain," Romeo told the sleeping Juliet, "with worms that are thy chambermaids." He embraced and kissed her, then took a bottle with a long stopper out of his pocket. He looked hard at the bottle. "Come, bitter conduct, come, unsavory guide!" he said.

Ju bit her lip. She knew that the bottle contained poison. Romeo seemed to be having trouble opening the bottle. He pulled and pulled at the stopper, then looked toward the tomb as if wondering whether to smash the bottle against the stone.

But of course, it was probably not real stone.

"Come, bitter conduct," he repeated, tugging at the stopper once more. He was beginning to turn red. "Come, unsavory guide!" he shouted, glaring into the wings as if the person responsible for the stuck stopper was waiting there.

Romeo tried again. The part of Jonquil that had threaded itself around the stopper and the bottle could no longer hold against the smooth glass. The stopper popped out. "Thou desperate pilot . . . ," Romeo said with feeling. He began to tip the poison into a gold cup that had been left in the tomb.

Judging that Romeo was about to drink the poison, Jonquil turned his attention to the girl. He rolled closer to her. "Wake up!" he shouted in her ear. But he had forgotten—humans could not detect his voice. He turned himself into a cone and poked her in the arm. "Gerroff!" she said between clenched teeth.

"Here's to my love!" cried Romeo. He lifted the gold cup to his lips.

There was no time to lose. Jonquil entwined himself round Juliet's hair and pulled.

"Ow!" she screamed, sitting bolt upright.

Romeo froze, the cup millimeters from his lip. He glued his eyes to the audience and began to edge the cup toward his mouth.

"Ow!" cried Juliet, more loudly this time.

Romeo turned to Juliet, meeting her fierce look. He lowered the cup.

"My . . . my love," he stammered. "Why Juliet, my wife! My love!"

Juliet continued to glare at him.

"Juliet, thou art not dead, but . . . livest."

"Aye," said Juliet frostily. "The good friar's potion has been most effective. I was only feigning death."

"Good job thou wakest in time," said Romeo, indicating the cup of poison.

A man in a brown robe came onto the stage, followed by the parents of Romeo and Juliet, their servants, several townspeople and the prince.

"Friar!" cried Romeo, like a drowning man spying a lifeboat.

The robed man came to the center of the stage. "I'll be brief," he said, and for once he was. "Romeo, there alive, is husband to that Juliet," he declared. "And she . . . there alive, that Romeo's faithful wife."

"Hooray!" cried one of the servants weakly. Juliet rose from her deathbed and embraced Romeo.

The audience began to applaud, uncertainly at first, then rising to a crescendo.

"Bravo!"

People rose, clapping as if their lives depended on it. A shout went up: "Director! Director!" A man in a baggy white shirt and trousers came onto the stage.

"So unexpected!" Marcia shouted to Fleur above the applause. "I told you he was avant-garde!"

Eager was busy clapping too, though he kept glancing at the seat in front for a sign of Jonquil. Meanwhile, the director bowed and gestured at the cast to include them in the acclaim.

Few people noticed that the prince, all of a sudden, was sporting a yellow feather in his cap.

CHAPTER 22

"I must congratulate Hans," said Marcia.

As Marcia forged her way through the departing audience, Fleur looked at Ju and Finbar. "Where's Eager?"

Finbar pointed to where they had been sitting. "Down there. I think he's looking for something."

Fleur leant over the nearest seat. "Eager!" The robot's head appeared.

"Marcia wants us to go backstage," said Fleur. "What are you doing?"

"I must have dropped the lexiscreen I was reading," said Eager.

"We left it in the foyer," said Ju.

Eager stood up. "Oh, yes, so we did."

"We'd better hurry," said Fleur.

The auditorium had emptied but for a few people chatting. Ju, Finbar and Eager followed Fleur onto the stage. Paris' sword, the gold cup, the glass bottle were ordinary at close range, but something hard to define hung over them, a leftover charge from the performance. Finbar gently kicked the side of the tomb.

"Plastic," he said.

"There you are!" cried his mother. She held the director by the arm. "Hans, this is my friend Fleur, my son, Finbar, and here . . . ," she said breathlessly, leading him toward Ju, "is the real Juliet!"

The director threw back his head and laughed. "No, really?" he said.

Ju was horror-struck. How dare Marcia reveal her name to everyone!

But the director was holding out his hand, and Ju had little choice but to take it. "Delighted to meet you," he said, squeezing hard. He turned and shouted, "Nurse! Come here!"

It took the woman a moment to amble onto the stage. She had not changed out of her costume. As she came nearer, Ju realized that she was an animat.

"Nurse, listen carefully," said the director. "This is Juliet. The *real* Juliet."

"Faith, I know her," said the animat. "She was the prettiest babe that e'er I nursed." She pinched Ju's cheek. "Why, lamb! Why, lady!"

Now everyone was laughing. Even her mother, Ju noticed with dismay, was suppressing a smile.

"Thank you, Juliet," said the director solemnly. "It is inspiring to meet a modern girl with this name. I have never met one before."

Ju tried to be gracious. "I was named after my dad's grand-mother," she mumbled.

The director nodded. "That's a lot to live up to—your great-grandmother and a spirited heroine. But I am sure you will."

A bell chimed from the jinn on his wrist. "A congratulatory message from Stockholm," said the jinn.

The director smiled apologetically as he left the stage. "The whole world seems to know that Juliet and Romeo live on!"

* * * * *

No one noticed Eager's antics while the director talked to Ju. The robot lifted up the corners of the rug that covered the tomb, and peered underneath. He went down on his hands and knees and paced the floor, like a sniffer dog.

It was not until he tipped the gold cup upside down and shook it that Finbar turned and saw him. "Still looking for something?"

"I . . . yes . . . no . . . I . . ."

"Uncle Eager," called a voice, which only Eager heard. He swung round.

"Now what's the matter?" said Finbar.

Eager rushed over to the nurse, who was leaving the stage. "Excuse me," he said, thrusting his hand into her apron pocket. The nurse gave a cry of alarm and struck Eager about the ears. He jumped back, but instead of feeling his head, as a person would have done, he appeared to be rubbing his shoulder.

"What were you doing?" said Fleur. "You're lucky she's an animat."

"She responded like a human," said Marcia with a laugh.

"I thought I saw something—"

"Eager, I think it's time to go home." Fleur took his arm.

Now that Jonquil was safely across his shoulders, Eager was happy to board the pod to the suburbs. He expected Jonquil to talk about the evening on the journey home, but his nephew was silent. "Jonquil is growing calmer," Eager thought. Marcia and Finbar went on to their hotel, and Fleur and Ju began walking. The lights were on in cafés, and music blared from gobeyhalls.

"I enjoyed that," said Ju. "I didn't expect to, but I did."

"I'm sorry about Marcia and the director," said Fleur.

"That's OK," said Ju. "At least Marcia didn't announce my name to the entire audience." They walked on in silence. "Juliet," repeated Ju experimentally. "It isn't quite me, but perhaps one day . . . Mum, do you think Dad would have enjoyed the play?"

"He loves the theater," said her mother. She sounded distracted. "Come on, let's walk a bit faster."

They turned down a narrow street lined with dark, shuttered shops. There was no one else about. Above them, a cloud glided across the face of the moon. Ju observed it sadly.

Another time, she would have told herself that her dad was watching the very same cloud, but now he was on the far side of the moon, the side that never saw Earth.

"Marcia said she hasn't seen Dad since your wedding. That means Dad has never met Finbar. . . ." Ju had the impression that her mum was only half-listening and fell silent.

As they walked on, Ju heard footsteps behind them, constantly stumbling. "A drunk," she thought. She glanced at her mum.

"This way," Fleur whispered, and pulled her into a small yard next to a shop. They pressed their backs against the wall. Fleur put a protective arm across Ju's chest. Ju held her breath. They waited in the dark for the footsteps to pass.

A bundled-up figure with an uncertain gait went by. The footsteps continued down the street. Ju breathed again, just as the footsteps stopped.

"Mistress? What lamb! What Juliet! Where's this girl?"

"It's the nurse," squealed Ju.

Her mother stepped out into the light. "Nurse!" she called.

"My lady . . ." The animat limped toward Fleur.

"Nurse," said Fleur sternly. "Thou shouldst not be abroad. Thou must return to the theater."

Ju looked at her mother in admiration for her sudden command of sixteenth-century English.

"Would you have me see a play, my lady?"

"The theater is where you belong," said Ju, speaking firmly like her mother.

The nurse staggered backward and put a hand to her heart. "The theater? Am I a painted woman? Am I a flirt-gill?"

"Of course you aren't," said Fleur hastily. "That isn't what she meant. But you must return to Lady Juliet."

The nurse put her hands on her ample hips. "Have I not been jauncing up and down to find her? Lord, how my head aches! Fie, how my bones ache!" She pointed a plump finger at Ju.

"And how does she greet me—'You belong in the theater!' Is this the poultice for my aching bones?"

"Omigod," said Ju. "She thinks I'm Juliet! It's all Marcia's fault, and that director! He told the nurse I was 'the real Juliet.' "

"Calm down," said her mother. "I'm sure we can sort this out. Nurse, thou art mistaken. This is not Lady Juliet. Lady Juliet awaits you in her bedchamber. Thou must return to . . . to whence thou came . . . camest."

The nurse did not stir.

"Well done, Mum," said Ju.

Fleur sighed. "There's nothing else for it, she'll have to come home with us tonight. I'll leave a message for the theater director to come and collect her tomorrow."

The three set off. Ju and Fleur had to adjust their step to the nurse's uneven walk, and put up with her grumbling over her aching bones and sore back, all the way to the dance school.

It took them a while to persuade the nurse to enter the glass-sided lift. " 'Tis a moving box, that's all," said Fleur.

"Fie, 'tis a conjuror's box," said the nurse.

"Wouldst thou prefer to walk five floors to the top?" said Ju.

The nurse crossed herself and followed them into the lift.

"Where shall we put her?" said Ju as they entered the house.

"Oh, no! She slept in Juliet's bedroom. But she is not coming into my room. Not now, not ever!"

Her mother smiled at her. "Don't worry. Come, Nurse," she called, going into the kitchen. "You can lie in here. It's warm." She winked at Ju. "I'll fetch a blanket."

"The floor's hard," said Ju.

"She's an animat. She won't feel a thing. Besides, she'll be in sleep mode." Fleur arranged a blanket on the floor. "Here, Nurse, next the oven."

Ju could tell that her mum was secretly enjoying herself. "Take care not to wake us in the morning, Nurse. Sleep well."

"Sleep tight, my lady. And you, Juliet, you lazy lamb, you slugabed."

"Good night," said Ju, thankfully leaving the kitchen.

CHAPTER 23

The following morning Ju woke early as usual. She had been so tired the night before that she had not closed the partition between her bedroom and the living area. From her bed, she could see onto the terrace. It looked like a sunny day, but the wind was buffeting the plants in the tubs.

She headed for the bathroom. When she came out, she could smell the aroma of freshly baked bread. Her mother met her in the hallway. "Morning, Ju," she said sleepily. "Are you warming bread?"

"There is no bread," said Ju. "I toasted the last bun yesterday."

Her mother dashed to the kitchen, Ju hurrying after her. The table was spread as if for a banquet. There were a huge bowl of fruit salad, pots of yogurt, jams and honey, small cakes crowned with almonds, and a loaf of bread with a shiny glaze. Next to the food were a jug of freshly squeezed orange juice and another of steaming hot chocolate.

"My goodness," gasped Fleur.

The nurse came over from the oven bearing a pan of scrambled eggs.

"Hurry, my lady! To table!" she cried.

Ju took her place opposite her mother. "I don't believe this," she said. The nurse spooned the brightest, fluffiest scrambled eggs she had ever seen onto her plate.

"How did you manage this?" said Fleur to the nurse.

The animat looked vacantly at her.

"I mean, how didst thou knoweth how to prepareth . . ." Fleur tried again. "How knowest you how to prepareth thith . . ."

"Let me try," said Ju, laughing. She spoke clearly and slowly: "How did you know what to do, Nurse? And where to find everything?"

The nurse put down the saucepan and crossed herself. "Oh, my lady, to think I am a sinner. I have not been shriven these six months. Marry, 'twas Shrove Tuesday last when I saw the priest. Yet he spoke to me. I wonder that he would—"

"Peace," cried Fleur. "Who spoke to you?"

The nurse crossed herself again. "God," she said.

Ju and Fleur exchanged baffled looks.

"Nurse," said a deep voice, "you've forgotten the butter. And have you fetched the mugs for the hot chocolate?"

"The gobetween told her!" said Ju, laughing.

The nurse crossed herself again and looked heavenward. "No. Forgive me, Lord." She hastened to a cupboard and brought two mugs over to the table.

"And the butter?" said the gobetween.

"In the cold chest, Lord?"

"That's right," said the gobetween.

"Now we know where to turn if we can't handle her." Fleur took a mouthful of scrambled egg. "Delicious!"

Ju said warily, "How can we have a problem handling her if she's not here, Mum? She's going back today, isn't she?"

"I managed to speak to the director last night," said Fleur. "He was still at the theater when I called—having a party. He said . . . mm, this hot chocolate is divine! Let me pour you some." She reached across for Ju's mug.

"He didn't say 'Mm, this hot chocolate is divine,' " said Ju crossly. "Come on, Mum, when is he collecting the nurse?"

"He explained all about the animats," said her mother. "It's fascinating! Apparently, it's very expensive to put on plays with large casts of people, which is why Shakespeare is so rarely performed. But now animats can play the minor characters. When they're built, they're programmed with the language and knowledge of a particular period. Then directors can program them with whatever text they want. Each animat can perform in several plays, as long as they're of the same period."

"Thank goodness," said Ju. "So the nurse is needed for another play."

"Well . . . no," said her mum. "There isn't a part for her in the next production. The director was going to use her in a crowd scene."

"She'll be wonderful."

"But he's more than happy for her to stay here. In fact," Fleur

128

said hastily, "he would prefer it. It'll be better for her, he said, to be fully operational."

"Fully operational?" said Ju, breaking off to listen to the nurse, who was singing about cuckoos as she tidied the kitchen.

"Is that what she is?"

Her mother said brightly, "What do you think?"

Ju put an elbow on the table and propped her face on her hand. "Mum, you know what I think."

The nurse bustled over to the table. "Mistress Juliet, shall I make up your bed?"

Ju looked up. "Er . . . yes." She saw that her mother was smiling archly at her.

CHAPTER 24

While Mr. and Mrs. Bell were having breakfast in the dining room, Eager took Jonquil into the garden and pointed out the boundaries between the Bells' house and their neighbors.

"Please stay this side of the fence," said Eager. "I don't know what you might encounter in the gardens next door. Dogs, cats . . ."

"I can run faster—" began Jonquil.

"Yes. But perhaps it's better to explore the unknown when I'm with you."

"All right," said Jonquil.

Eager went back into the house and joined the Bells.

"That play you saw last night has hit the headlines," said Mr. Bell as he sipped his coffee. "The house told me it was on the news, and sure enough—" He handed Eager a lexiscreen. "I put it on the lexiscreen for you."

"Thank you," said Eager, taking the slim box from Mr. Bell.

His eyes scanned the page: "Stunningly original production," he read. ". . . The play's director, Hans Rutter, says 'Theater without risk is dead theater.' "

"I'm surprised no one's changed the ending before," said Mr. Bell. "Nearly five hundred years of performances, and it's been retold endless ways—different periods, different countries. There are musicals and films. I believe there's even a gobeyhall version where you can *be* Romeo or Juliet—but it's never had a happy ending till now."

"It is supposed to be a tragedy," said Mrs. Bell.

"Last night sounds more of a comedy. Is that right, Eager?" said Mr. Bell.

Eager was reading the line: "Juliet, waking with a scream as if she had been bitten by a particularly nasty bedbug . . ."

"Eager?" repeated Mr. Bell.

The robot was gazing into the air. Then—"Excuse me," he said, bolting from the room. Mrs. Bell waited until the door had closed behind him.

"I wish he wouldn't do that," she said, sighing.

"Do what?"

"Stare into space like that. It isn't like him. I'm beginning to think he's breaking down."

Mr. Bell set down his coffee cup and looked at his wife with sympathy. "Chloe, if one of our children did the same, what would you have thought?"

"I'd have thought they were worried about something. Or that they had something to hide."

"And why should Eager be any different?" he said meaning-fully.

Mrs. Bell gazed from her husband to the door and back again. "Hmm."

※　※　※　※　※

Eager stood in the garden at the back of the house, calling for Jonquil. He thought of a picture that Gavin had once shown him, of women in brightly colored dresses who strapped their babies to their bodies with lengths of cloth. Perhaps carrying Jonquil on his back, or having him in sight at all times, was the only way to keep his nephew out of trouble.

"Jonquil!" he called. A bunch of leaves plopped down from the tree beside him, landing with a dry crackle. The leaves turned prematurely golden.

"Jonquil," said Eager. "About last night . . ."

The leaves formed a thin sheet and hopped across the grass toward him. "That's what I wanted to talk to you about, Uncle Eager."

"About Juliet?" said Eager.

"She's sad," said Jonquil, "but not sad and confused like the boy."

"Which boy? Romeo?" asked Eager, beginning to feel con-fused himself.

"No, the other boy. The son who came with his mother."

"Marcia's son," said Eager, realizing that Jonquil must be

talking about Ju and Finbar. "How do you know what Finbar is feeling?"

"I see it," said Jonquil, balancing on one corner. "You know that I see things inside a machine, by entering the circuitry. It's the same with people. I look inside them and know what they are feeling."

"You go inside them?" said Eager.

"Not inside their skin," said Jonquil. He gave a pirouette. "Inside the field that surrounds them."

Eager pondered this. He sensed, himself, that all things had a force around them, which was especially strong for humans and animals and plants. He went closer to the tree and, sure enough, he picked up a frequency that he knew belonged to it.

"Finbar's field told you that he is sad and confused?"

"Yes. I saw it last night."

Eager recalled that the boy had been very quiet. He had sat waiting for Ju and Fleur with downcast eyes.

"Why does he feel like that?" said Eager.

"Because of his clothes," said Jonquil.

"People don't feel sad and confused because of their clothes," Eager said.

"Lori Jones does," said Jonquil, "all the time." He hopped back across the grass toward Eager. "And money. He's worried about money."

Eager tilted his head. "I think Marcia is rich. I don't know why he should be worried. Are you sure?"

"I saw the worry," insisted Jonquil. "It looked like this . . ."

He became a ball, a twisted knot of a ball with sharp protruding spikes.

"Poor Finbar," said Eager. "No wonder he seemed unhappy. You said Ju was sad?"

"That's right," said Jonquil. "But it's a simple sadness. She knows why, and that it will end. It feels like this. . . ." He hopped to the stone seat at the end of the garden and draped himself over the edge, like a well-wrung rag hung out to dry.

"I understand," said Eager. "Can you see everyone's field?"

In reply, the rag unraveled into a single thread, which began to spin round on itself, faster and faster. Strands of Jonquil were flying everywhere, until they were caught in the vortex.

The whirling mass grew larger, changing colors from red, yellow and pink, to green and blue, purple and orange.

"That's Marcia!" cried Eager.

The vortex slowed, and the alternating colors merged into Jonquil's golden hue. Eager was curious to see the energies of all his friends, but there were more important things on his mind. "If Ju and Finbar are sad, we must help them," he said. "But how do we know what the problem is?"

CHAPTER 25

Finbar passed such a deep dreamless night that he wondered whether he had slept at all. He must have closed his eyes for a second and opened them again. Yet he felt refreshed, and when he leant out of bed to pluck at the end of the curtain, a sharp ray of light was released into the room.

He crawled back under the bedclothes, enjoying the feeling of a new day, until he remembered. He had still not found the courage to tell his mother about the thief.

He had worn the dreadful clothes to the theater, hoping to appall her so that it would be easier to confess. But Marcia had been thrilled, swooping down with cries of "Darling, you look wonderful!"

A day had passed since the theft. Who knew what the thief had got up to by now? Finbar groaned and reached for his jinn on the bedside table. He pressed the button to turn on the gobetween. "Gobey, open the curtains," he said.

Sunlight flooded the room, making Finbar blink. "Jinn, show me my account." The numbers that scrolled down the tiny screen were unchanged from the day before. His relief was short-lived.

"All that money for one horrible suit," he thought.

He was dressing when his mother knocked on the door. She kissed him good morning. "Did you sleep well?"

"Like a log, Mum. I'm ready for breakfast."

She went over to the sofa opposite the bed and sat down, patting the space beside her. "Finbar, there's something very important I want to say to you."

Finbar's breath caught in his throat. His skin turned clammy. She knew about the thief! His legs were on autopilot as he walked over and sat beside her.

"I don't know how it happened."

His mother seemed not to have heard. She said, "I noticed how you watched Eager at the Bells' house, and again at the theater last night. I know you're trying to figure him out, so I've decided to tell you the truth. The Bells might not agree with me, but you're old enough now, and I know you can be trusted."

Finbar struggled to follow her.

"And another thing," she continued. "It's better to tell you than leave you to puzzle things out for yourself. You might end up asking questions of the wrong people."

"Mum, I've no idea what you're talking about."

"Of course you haven't." She stood up and walked to the window, where the light made a halo of her thick chestnut hair. "What do you know about the Ban?"

"The Ban . . ." Finbar searched his memory. "It's the law that every government has passed, to stop scientists from building conscious robots," he said.

"Very good," said his mother. "Do you know what that means?"

He thought for a moment. "Not really."

"As you know, we've had robots of one kind or another for a hundred years," said Marcia. "In that time they've grown more intelligent—that's to say, they can make sense of the physical world, reason, take decisions . . ."

"Like the animats," said Finbar. "They're the most intelligent robots we have."

Marcia gave an ironic laugh. "Do you think the animats are intelligent?"

Finbar said defensively, "Well, they are, for machines. They can do all the things you mentioned. But they're not intelligent like humans. They don't really understand anything. They can't . . ." He searched for the right word. "They can't reflect on what they do."

"You've put it very well," said his mother, coming to sit next to him again. "But years ago, scientists weren't content with that sort of intelligence. They thought if robots could understand human emotions, they would understand people, and the world, better. They tried all kinds of experiments. LifeCorp—you know about LifeCorp?"

"Of course. They build the animats, and Granddad used to work for them."

"Yes," said Marcia. "LifeCorp tried to make self-aware robots—"

Finbar interrupted. "I've read stories about that sort of thing. Could they really do it?"

Marcia gave a wry smile. "I was skeptical too at your age. Now you can only read about it as fiction, because the science has been banned. If you write about it, or worse still, try to put it into practice, you risk a long time in prison."

"The Ban," said Finbar.

His mother nodded. "Every scientist or technocrat has to agree to it. They won't get a job otherwise."

"But why?" asked Finbar. "Something must have happened. . . . Did the robots from LifeCorp go wrong?"

"Badly wrong. LifeCorp took a shortcut, you see. They gave their robots human memories. . . ."

"That sounds creepy," said Finbar.

"Well, it worked for a time, but then the robots went out of control. The gobetween will tell you about it—it's no secret. I'm explaining about the Ban so that you understand how serious this is."

Finbar frowned. "What exactly are you telling me, Mum?"

Marcia stood up again. "When LifeCorp built these robots, another scientist called Professor Ogden and his team were building Eager. They took a completely different approach; they designed him to learn from his experiences, and to feel emotions."

"Emotions?" Finbar whistled. "An emotional robot . . ." He

remembered Eager at the Bells' house, frantically peering under the kitchen table, and again at the theater, delving into the nurse's apron. He laughed. "Perhaps that's what the robot was searching for last night—his lost emotions!"

"Whatever are you talking about?"

He shrugged. "It's just, whenever I see him, he appears to be looking for something."

"I've no idea what that's about," said Marcia. "Most of the time Eager's in hiding. He only leaves his home to visit the Bells once a year. Perhaps he's forgetting how to behave in public. . . ." She fell silent and looked sad suddenly.

"I think I understand what you're saying," said Finbar. "Eager *is* different. He looks at you as if he really sees you, not like the animats—they have cold, blank eyes, even when they're smiling." He thought for a moment and added, "It's still hard to believe."

"That's the problem," his mother said. "The entire world finds it hard to believe. It's more than that. . . ." She sat on the bed and leant toward him. Her tone became passionate.

"People are scared, Finbar! They're afraid that if robots can feel like us, they'll feel all the dangerous things, such as anger and greed, and the urge to be cruel. . . . Then they'll start to compete with us, and because they're machines, they'll prove stronger than us and will take over."

"It could happen, couldn't it?"

"Why should it?" demanded Marcia. "Eager has never behaved cruelly. He might retaliate if someone attacked him, or threatened one of the Bells, or someone else he cared about. . . . But Eager wouldn't lie or steal or harm or kill for the reasons we do. What people forget is this—"

Her eyes flashed. "They forget that humans took two million years to evolve. Most of that time we lived in the wild, at the mercy of predators and the elements. We fought over food, mates and shelter. Our primitive urges still affect how we behave today. Like animals, we fear being hungry, alone, cold, homeless, even when we're surrounded by all this." She gestured at the hotel room.

"Not everyone stays in a five-star hotel," thought Finbar; but he understood his mother's point. People, whether rich or poor, were afraid of not having things.

"Robots have none of these instincts," she said. "There's no reason for them to behave threateningly, unless in self-preservation. Robots like Eager want to enjoy life alongside us, not destroy it."

"If you say so," thought Finbar. Aloud he said, "But what if robots are threatened? Or if they get confused and just think they're being threatened? Then they might harm us."

"It's a risk," said his mother, "but a very small one." She lifted her chin. "Remember, I'm a technocrat's daughter. I understand these things."

Finbar smiled to himself. "A risk is still a risk," he ventured to say.

To his surprise, his mother relaxed. She came back to the sofa and placed an arm around him. "Finbar, darling, we put our lives into the hands of machines every day—in hospitals, in the street, in our homes. Machines that have no idea what makes us tick. Think of the damage they could do if they went wrong. So we have safeguards in place to stop them causing harm, and people trust that the safeguards will work."

"Are you saying we should do the same with conscious robots?" said Finbar. "But how can you keep a check on robots with the freedom to do what they want?" It was hard enough keeping track of Eager, let alone thousands like him.

Marcia stood up and pulled him to his feet. "By living alongside them and keeping an eye on them, in case one of them goes berserk." She turned at the door and said laughingly, "Just as we do with humans!"

CHAPTER 26

As Finbar followed his mother to the dining room, he came to a resolution. He would tell her about the theft. It was time to get it off his chest. He waited until they took their seats.

"Mum," he began.

The animat-waiter came for their order. "Tea with lemon," said Marcia. "And toast."

"A boiled egg," said Finbar. "And croissants."

"I called Fleur this morning," said Marcia, raising her voice against the rain beating on the windows. "We'd like to see an exhibition today. Do you want to come?"

"Not really."

"We thought not. You and Ju could entertain yourselves here, in the pool or the gobeyhall."

"OK," said Finbar with mixed feelings. He welcomed Ju's company, but she was bound to ask about his new clothes. The thought reminded him of his intention.

"I've got something to tell you," he said.

"Have you?" His mother was squeezing lemon juice into her tea. "Oh, let me tell you something first! Fleur and Ju have adopted the nurse."

"What?"

Marcia recounted the events of the previous night. "Hans said the nurse can stay with them," she concluded.

Fleur and Ju appeared, crossing the room pursued by an animat-waiter, who took their wet coats.

Ju said, "We've had an amazing breakfast."

"Scrumdelicious, as Sam would say!" said her mum.

Ju and Fleur laughed together and started talking about the nurse. What a transformation had come over them! Until now they had looked downcast whenever Sam's name was mentioned.

※ ※ ※ ※ ※

When their mothers left, Ju and Finbar sat in an uncomfortable silence. Finbar sensed that Ju was dying to hear the story behind the turquoise suit. The longer she resisted asking, the more Finbar warmed to her. He said apologetically, "Perhaps we could swim later. I'm too full now."

"Me too," said Ju. "You should have seen the nurse's breakfast. I can't believe an animat can cook so well."

"How long is she going to stay with you?"

"Until the theater needs her, I suppose," said Ju. "Yesterday I wanted her to go back straightaway. But I want her to stay for

Mum's sake. She made the beds this morning, and now she's cleaning and doing the washing. The gobetween tells her how to do everything. It's very funny." She began to fiddle with a napkin. "Mum's so relaxed today. You see, with Dad gone, she has to do everything herself. I try to help, but Mum still feels she has to look after me." She bit on her lip. "This isn't the first time my dad's been sent away—not to the moon, but still a long way away. Mum says it's because he won't toe the scientific line, whatever that means."

Finbar thought about the conversation with his mother that morning. He wanted to ask more about this "scientific line," but Ju went on, "Mum says your dad goes away a lot too."

Finbar nodded. "By choice, not because of his job."

"Does your mum miss him?"

"They're not really together anymore," said Finbar. "They only see each other because of me. I didn't want to come on this trip, because I should be spending this month with my dad. But he wanted to go on a retreat and Mum wanted to bring me here, so . . ."

They fell silent again.

"I like your mum," said Ju. "She's lively."

"So are conger eels," said Finbar.

Ju giggled. "What are her paintings like? We've got a pottery bowl she gave to Mum and Dad as a wedding present. I love the colors."

"Her pictures are bright too," said Finbar. "I can show you them."

Ju glanced around the dining room as if she might find an original Marcia Morris on the walls.

"An exhibition has just opened in Amsterdam," said Finbar. "I can take you. On the gobey, that is."

Ju's eyes went to the window, where the rain was still lashing down. "Do we have to go out?"

"No," said Finbar. "There's a gobeyhall downstairs."

*   *   *   *   *

The gobeyhall itself was booked for a wedding reception.

"There's a smaller room at the side you can use," said the clerk.

"Is it three-D?" said Finbar.

"Of course, sir."

The room was rectangular, with a high ceiling. "Perfect," said Finbar. "Gobey, take us to the Jackson Gallery in Amsterdam."

"So the gallery's shut today?" said Ju as they waited to be connected.

"No," said Finbar.

"But gobey visits are normally out of hours," said Ju. "Otherwise you'd be looking at the people visiting the museum or gallery without their permission. It's not allowed. . . ."

Finbar grinned. "Believe it or not, some people enjoy being

watched. They even dress up for it. So every Sunday this gallery lets gobey visitors come at the same time as the public."

"And they don't mind that we can see them but they can't see us?" said Ju.

"Apparently not."

The four sides of the room began to pulse with light. Blurred shapes loomed onto the screens. Finbar and Ju stepped to the center of the room, while the shapes took form as painted canvases against a white background.

"It starts here," said Finbar, pointing to where the door had been, which was now part of the screen.

Ju said nothing for a moment or two as she stared at the first paintings. Then, "They're wonderful," she said quietly.

Finbar looked pleased.

Ju had half-expected Marcia to use bold splashes of color, but the pictures said so much with so little. A few colors sweeping and overlapping across the canvas, and Ju was transported to different places and climates.

"That's the sea!" she said, pointing to a swirl of red, orange, yellow and gray. "The sea at sunset."

Finbar walked beside her, without comment, except to confirm Ju's guesses. When they reached the far end, the paintings on either side slid away and new ones took their place. Finally, Ju turned her attention to a larger painting.

"It's you!" she cried. It showed a figure in a garden. A brown smudge above a block of white captured the tilt of Finbar's head when he was sitting and thinking.

"That's not me," said Finbar's voice from behind her.

"Yes it is," she insisted.

"It's not me!" Ju swung round. Finbar had his back to her, facing the other end of the gallery. She went to stand beside him and noticed that he was pale, his jaw clenched. A boy had just arrived at the gallery and was shaking hands with a man and a woman at the reception desk.

An animat came up to the boy with a tray and offered him a drink. The adults were smiling and asking him questions and listening to his replies with rapt attention.

"That isn't me." Finbar's voice was a low rumble, like a storm about to break.

"Of course it isn't," said Ju. She looked at the boy again, taking in his lurid red shirt and striped trousers. "It's one of those people you told me about who like to dress up and be watched on the gobetween."

Finbar kept his eyes on the boy. "That's how I'm greeted at my mum's exhibitions."

Ju frowned. She had not imagined Finbar to be the jealous type. He went on, deliberately, "And this is my mum's exhibition."

Ju exclaimed, "You think he's pretending to be you?"

"I know he is."

Ju walked toward the reception area and stared long and hard at the boy. She knew that he was unable to see her, but it felt as if he had only to look straight ahead and his eyes would meet hers.

The boy was tall, pasty-faced. It would be hard to remember his features exactly. But there was nothing forgettable about his clothes. The gaudy colors struck a chord with her.

"I get it," she said. "He's a friend of yours who likes wearing strange clothes. You borrowed his turquoise suit to wear to the theater, and now he's in Amsterdam pretending to be you." She turned to Finbar. "Is it some sort of game?"

Finbar was shaking his head. "The suit is mine. At least, Mum paid for it. But *he* ordered it from Whittaker and Co. And we're not friends. I don't even know his name!"

He fell to his knees and struck his forehead against the padded floor several times. Ju was both aghast and admiring. She had never seen anyone do this for real.

"I hate him!" Finbar cried. "How dare he pretend to be me! How dare he steal from me!"

"What are you talking about?" said Ju, nervous. She took a step toward him. "Look, let's go. Then you can tell me what's happened."

Finbar leant back on his heels and took a deep breath. He stood up. "Gobey, switch off," he said calmly.

The paintings, the gallery and the boy faded into nothing. Finbar watched them disappear, his lips tightly drawn. He glanced sideways at Ju. "Sorry," he said. As the door opened for them, he faced her. "Do you know what I hate him for most?"

Ju pretended to think. "His dress sense?"

Finbar grinned. "How did you guess?"

148

CHAPTER 27

The hotel lounge had round chairs that molded themselves to the shape of the sitter. Some guests had curled up in them, like nesting birds. Others sprawled backward, as if caught in midair by a giant mitten. But Finbar and Ju perched on the edges of their seats as they leant toward each other conspiratorially.

"You're saying the boy in the gallery is the one you met on the Sorbjet," said Ju. "But you'd never seen him before?"

"Never," said Finbar.

"And you lent him your jinn. . . ."

"I'm an idiot!"

"You wanted to help him," said Ju. "I wouldn't give my jinn to someone in the street in case they ran off with it. But on a plane there's nowhere to go."

"That's what I thought," said Finbar. "Or I would have, if I'd stopped to think."

Ju raised her eyebrows. "What a way to repay you! He breaks into your mum's account and steals a suit."

"And what he's wearing today, I bet," said Finbar. "I've been puzzled by how much he spent. I bet he bought himself a whole new wardrobe, which might explain why he hasn't used the account since."

She said tentatively, "But what makes you think he's stolen your identity?"

"He turned up at the gallery and claimed to be me—"

"You don't know that," interrupted Ju. "You're only guessing."

"I could tell he got the red-carpet treatment."

"Well, I've never had a famous mother so I wouldn't know." She chewed her lip. "I still don't see how he took information from your jinn. Not in ten minutes, not on a plane full of people."

"I don't know how either. But I think he downloaded it," said Finbar. "How else would he know enough to steal from me and turn up at the exhibition?"

"Jinns are like minigobeys. They know everything about their owners," said Ju. "You can't break a jinn's code just like that."

"Hackers can," said Finbar. "Hackers are always one step ahead of the technology."

"What exactly *is* a hacker?"

Finbar lowered his voice. "Technocrats on the wrong side of the law. They understand the technology and use it for their own ends, but they don't have regular jobs." He put his head between his hands. "I should never have given him my jinn."

"But where did he download it? Onto what?"

Finbar shrugged. "Another jinn? They could have done it in seconds if they knew what they were doing."

"They?"

"I don't know why I said that. . . ." Finbar thought for a moment. "He's my age. He must have an accomplice." He bowed his head again. "It doesn't make sense, though. He couldn't have known that I was going to talk to him, much less offer him my jinn. So he can't have planned it all."

"But he grabbed the chance and he knew what to do, so he must be a proper thief," said Ju.

Finbar looked up. "Wait a minute. We were floating; he bumped into me. Perhaps it was deliberate. . . ."

"Finbar!" said Ju. She was worried that he was working himself into a state again. "Does this matter?"

"I suppose not," he said. "I just want to know what I'm up against—one boy or a whole gang."

Ju said firmly, "You're not up against anything. All you have to do is tell your mum and she'll tell the police. They can arrest the boy—we know where he is now—and if he was impersonating you today, the gallery people are witnesses." She could see from the look on his face that Finbar was not convinced. "What's wrong?"

"I'm still puzzled. When he came back with the jinn, I thought he'd been to the viewing platform. I expected him to talk about it. But he just asked about my mum. Why did he do that?"

"Curiosity?"

"What if this is part of a bigger plot, to steal her paintings? I know it sounds ridiculous. . . ."

"All that from a chance meeting with you on a Sorbjet?" said Ju.

Finbar groaned. "You're right. My imagination has gone into hyperdrive. But why did he go to the gallery today?"

"If there is a plot," said Ju eagerly, "all the more reason to go to the police."

He gave a hollow laugh. "I'm having enough trouble persuading you. What will the police say? I can't even prove he stole the clothes, though I bet they all fit him perfectly. Why should they believe he's impersonating me?" He checked himself. "No, you're right. I'll tell Mum this evening. I was going to tell her at breakfast just now."

"Wait, I've thought of something," said Ju. An animat-waiter came over to them with a drinks menu. Finbar waved him away.

Ju dropped her voice. "I'm going to talk to my dad tomorrow. I can ask his advice. He's a technocrat, he's brilliant—he installed the gobey in our house so that it runs everything. He'll know the best thing to do."

Finbar's face lit up. "Do you think he will? You see, it's all my fault. I'd feel better if I could do something to help."

"I'm sure Dad will know all about hackers and identity theft," said Ju. "I'll call you in the afternoon, if you can wait that long, and tell you what he said."

Finbar looked downcast. "What if the boy uses my account in the meantime?"

"Can't you close it?"

"Not without my mum's permission."

Ju thought for a moment. "You just said he's got enough clothes to be going on with. And he probably thinks you've closed the account already. It's only one more day. . . ."

"You're right," said Finbar.

"Ju!" "Finbar!" Marcia and Fleur came across the lounge.

"Thanks, Ju," said Finbar, and she winked.

CHAPTER 28

As Eager and Mr. Bell left the house, Mrs. Bell called, "Good luck." The learning center that Mr. Bell had designed was to be fitted with its roof that morning. Mr. Bell talked to Eager about the project, excitedly, all the way to the bus stop.

"The entire roof will sit on millions of carbon nanotubes—each so thin that it's invisible to the naked eye. The top of the building will look as if it's floating in the air! Behind the tubes we'll put a transparent membrane. We don't want the rain and cold coming in," he said with a laugh.

Eager tried to imagine the ultrathin carbon tubes and thought of Jonquil's fibers. They had the same material at their core and were a hundred times stronger than steel. Could his nephew hold the weight of a roof?

"A very small one," said Jonquil's voice from across his shoulders.

"Gavin is joining us," said Mr. Bell as they reached the bus stop. "He's taken time off this week. He wants to see as much of you as he can. And of Molly, no doubt. She's here on holiday."

"I like Molly," said Eager.

"So do we. But Chloe and I have learnt not to build up our hopes. . . . Here's the bus."

Eager was curious about these hopes, but before he could ask, the hoverbus had dived down to the curb. It was one of the newer, saucerlike models. It was years since he had traveled on public transport. The Bells had thought it safer to keep him away from curious eyes, but after his successful outing to the theater, they were less cautious. A brown-suited animat nodded and let them pass.

"Travel is free now," said Mr. Bell in response to Eager's surprised look. "When cheap fuel became available there was such a rush of people buying cars that the roads grew congested, just like the old days. So the government introduced free public transport. No doubt we pay for it in taxes, but it's a lot more enjoyable for traveling about town."

The seats were arranged in concentric circles around a large domed machine that showed the route they were following.

"Please keep out of the dome," said Eager in his thoughts.

"I could put us on a quicker route," said Jonquil.

"No, thank you," thought Eager firmly. The other people on the bus did not look as if they would appreciate a detour.

Eager and Mr. Bell got off at the next stop. The river was ahead of them, sluggish and pale gray despite the sunshine. On the bank was the new learning center, boarded up like a hastily wrapped birthday present.

A security guard greeted them. "This is my personal assistant," Mr. Bell said. "And I'm Mr. Bell junior," said a voice behind them. Gavin held out his jinn for the animat to scan.

The learning center had three stories, and was rectangular, with the rounded edges that were typical of Mr. Bell's designs.

"Are the nanotubes on top?" said Eager.

"There are columns of them all the way round. Cross-braced to take the weight of the roof," said Mr. Bell. He stroked his jaw. "This is probably the most ambitious thing I've ever built, Eager. It's a metaphor, a picture of our times," he said. "Since it's a learning center, I thought of lifting the roof. The lid is off, so to speak, on knowledge and information. Because we all have the freedom to access information today, not only at learning centers but in our own homes."

"You're letting in the light too," Eager said.

"That's right. The light of knowledge, or truth. Yes, truth. The light of truth." Mr. Bell was silent for a moment.

"You're turning into a philosopher, Dad," said Gavin.

Mr. Bell laughed. "I'd better not. I've a building to complete." He led the robot and Gavin to the side of the building. "Those cranes over there are about to raise the roof!"

Four huge robotic cranes were at each corner of a protective cover the size of a liveball pitch. Several people in overalls stood in discussion beside the cranes. Eager had visited many of Mr. Bell's projects over the years, and he took a keen interest in his work. He approached the nearest crane. It gave a click and swiveled an optic sensor toward him.

"Hello," Eager said. "It must be a very large roof, under this cover. Who gives you the order to lift it?" The sensor whirled in the direction of the crane opposite and returned to face Eager.

"It does," said the crane.

Eager felt a pummeling across his shoulders. "What do you want?" he said aloud.

"Nothing," said the crane. "I want for nothing."

"I want to see the crane that gives the orders," said Jonquil's voice.

Eager walked along the side of the roof. "Hello," he said to the second crane. The crane neither spoke nor moved. Eager stood there for a minute.

"It's all right, Uncle Eager," said Jonquil. "We can go now."

"What did you do?" said Eager. As far as he could tell, his nephew had stayed on his shoulders.

"I checked its coordinates with those of the first crane. They fit," said Jonquil. "Can we go to the others?"

Eager stretched the rubber rings of his legs as he paced the perimeter of the roof. Why was Jonquil examining the cranes? Had he picked up on a fault, or was he merely curious?

"Is anything wrong?" Eager said.

Jonquil did not answer. At the last crane, Eager glimpsed a pair of cilia-wings flying over his shoulder. "The cranes are all right," Jonquil said.

"Why did you think something was the matter?" said Eager.

"I don't know. I only knew that I had to check."

"We should warn Mr. Bell if there's a problem." Eager followed Gavin into the site office, where Mr. Bell and his colleagues had begun to make final checks on the data for the placing of the roof. They stood peering at the screens of several gobetweens.

"Uncle Eager," said Jonquil's voice from Eager's shoulders. "Come and join me. I'm in the gobetween at the end."

Eager went to the machine, where no one else was standing, and looked at the rows of calculations on the screen. "What are those red lines?" he said.

"They're me," said Jonquil. "I'm underlining the calculation that I'm following."

A new red line appeared. Encircling a figure in the center of the screen, it began to flash. "And here is where the mistake has ended up," said Jonquil. "A very small mistake. A hundred-thousandth of a degree. But when you are using carbon nanotubes a little mistake is very big."

"A hundred-thousandth of a degree is tiny," said Eager.

"But all the nanotubes will be affected, so they may not hold up the roof." Eager recoiled in horror at the image of Mr. Bell's roof crashing down. "It might not crash," said Jonquil. "But if it sits wrongly on the nanotubes they may buckle."

Eager tilted his head and considered what to do. He zipped up to Mr. Bell. "Mr. Bell, have you checked the machine at the end?"

"Not today," said Mr. Bell. "Those calculations were

important when we put the nanotubes in place, but we don't need them now."

"Aren't you basing the new calculations on the old information?" said Eager.

"Yes," said Mr. Bell. He looked keenly at the robot. "What is this, Eager? Have you spotted something?"

"I happened to notice that one of the calculations is a hundred-thousandth of a degree out."

Mr. Bell hurried over to the gobetween. A technician, who had overheard Eager, joined him. "I can't see anything wrong," said Mr. Bell. His colleague shook her head.

"It's there." Eager pointed at the middle of the screen. But the red circle had disappeared, and all he saw was a sea of numbers.

"Down, up . . . across . . . down a bit," said Jonquil's voice. Eager's forefinger wavered until he found the figure.

"It looks all right to me," said the technician.

Eager began to wonder whether he was worrying Mr. Bell needlessly. "A hundred-thousandth of a degree is very small, isn't it? I don't expect it matters much."

"It wouldn't matter if just one joint between the nanotubes was a fraction out. But these columns are made up of millions of tubes, and the mistake will be magnified," said the woman.

"Let's see," said Mr. Bell. "If a million tubes are out by a hundred-thousandth of a degree each, then the top of the columns would be out by . . ."

"Ten degrees," said Jonquil to Eager.

"Ten degrees!" said the woman. "The columns could buckle under the load of the roof." She turned to Eager. "Where did you first pick up the mistake?"

Eager fixed his eyes on the screen as if trying to locate the spot.

"Top row, seventh number," said Jonquil.

Eager pointed to it. "The decimal point is in the wrong place!" cried the woman. "And it's been carried all the way down."

Mr. Bell straightened up. "This could have been very serious."

Gavin came over to them, a mug of tea in his hand. "Are you all right, Dad? You're pale."

"Not as pale as I would have been in an hour or two." Mr. Bell turned back to the screen, his face long. "If it wasn't for Eager, I'd be ruined."

"Ruined?" said Gavin, looking quizzically at the robot.

"Ruined!" cried Jonquil in Eager's ear. "That's just what Mr. Jones would say. I knew things would get more interesting around here."

CHAPTER 29

The windows of the dance school were open, and though it was lunchtime, the sound of piano music spilled onto the street, accompanied by the thud of feet on wooden floors.

As she went by, Ju heard a snatch of conversation from a side room.

"Did you watch *Stars in Space*?" said a girl's voice. "The actor who played Brock Jones won the mooncarting race."

"Brock Jones! He's so brave," said a second girl.

"He's just a stupid tourist," Ju thought. "My dad's the brave one, living up there." She felt like shouting this through the window, but it would be a waste of time.

She ran to the lift. The seconds that she was airborne felt like an eternity. She huffed impatiently for the moment it took the front door to recognize her. Inside the house she kicked off her shoes and heard voices. Her fantasy of the last few weeks had taken root in reality. Both her parents were there, laughing together!

She peered into the living area. Her mum, the touch-mantle across her shoulders, was facing her dad on the gobetween screen.

"Almost the real thing," said Ju to herself. Of course, she had known that her father was going to call, but it was still unsettling to arrive in the middle of the day and hear his voice, just as she had been imagining. She crept by so as not to interrupt them, intending to take a quick shower. "Ju!" her mother called. She went into the living area.

"Hi, Dad," she said.

His face lit up. "Come and join us."

She looked at her mother, in case she wanted longer alone with him. Fleur shook her head. "Sam's tired," she said. "Come and have a family hug."

Fleur shared the mantle with her. They laughed as Sam squeezed his arms.

"Well?" he said. "Does it work?"

"Kind of," said Ju. "How was your trip to the far side?"

Her father grinned. "Amazing. Better than last time. I could take more of it in." He leant forward. "Did you enjoy your weekend?"

Ju was about to reply when beside her she felt her mother stiffen. "Sam! What's happened to your necklace?"

"My . . . ?" Ju's father looked nonplussed.

"Your lucky stone. You never take it off," said Fleur.

He put his hand to his neck. "Didn't I put it back on? I had to take it off at the listening station. No one can wear anything that might interfere with the equipment. Just shows you how tired I am!"

"We'd better let you get some sleep," said Fleur.

"I'll just talk to Ju," said Sam. "How was the dinner at the Bells'?"

"It was good," said Ju. "Uncle Gavin has a new girlfriend called Molly."

"She's an astrobiologist," said Fleur. "She works for the International Space Authority too. I didn't catch her last name, but it's a small world, isn't it? Have you met her?"

"I can't recall her," Sam said, "but I'm so tired."

Fleur stood up. "I'll leave you," she said. "Can you call again tonight, after you've had a sleep?"

Her husband gave a knowing smile. "You want to check that I'm OK, and not suffering from space sickness. I'm sure ground control will let me. I'll speak to you later. Bye, Blossom." This was his pet name for his wife.

Ju checked that her mum had left the room, and leant closer to the screen. "Dad, there's something important I've got to ask you. My friend Finbar needs your advice."

Her father rubbed his eyes. "Can we talk about it later, Ju? I promise to hear all about it when I call tonight."

"But you said you wanted to talk. . . ." Ju checked herself. She knew she was being unfair. "OK, Dad. I'm sorry you're exhausted."

He smiled wanly. "Till later, then. Bye, Ju."

"Bye, Dad."

He faded away. Ju went behind the partition and sat on her bed. She told her jinn to connect her to Finbar and chewed her lip. Would Finbar want to wait any longer before telling Marcia about the thief? When his face appeared on the jinn, she burst out, "Dad's so tired. He was all right most of the time, but suddenly he'd say he was exhausted, so I don't think he'd have been able to think very clearly. . . ."

"Ju, don't worry!" said Finbar. "Mum and I are visiting friends and I can't talk to her until tonight anyway. So call me when you've spoken to your dad again."

"OK," said Ju, relieved. As Finbar's face disappeared, she imagined her dad, refreshed after a sleep, listening to the problem. She felt proud that he would be able to help.

CHAPTER 38

Ju had promised her mother that if she stayed home for the afternoon, she would study. But it was hard to concentrate on maths problems. She switched to her history project on Peter the Great, but tales of him building ships and cutting off beards could not hold her attention.

"Gobey, take me back to my story about the huntress."

The muddy-faced girl appeared, sitting some distance from a group of people, dressed in furs. Above them loomed a dark cloud. The hilly terrain was dotted with fallen boulders and sparsely covered in shrubs.

The people in the background were hacking at the carcass of an animal. Though the girl cast covert glances at them, they paid no attention to her. Meanwhile, her hands were busy with a stone, chipping pieces off a flatter, slate-colored stone to form a sharp edge.

The girl paused in her work to steal another look at the hunters. When they continued to ignore her, she stood up and took a few steps toward them. A cry rang out: a man was beating his chest and with his other hand pointing at her. As she came nearer, a rock landed at her feet. She ran back to the spot where she had been sitting, gathered up her spear and headed over the nearest grassy bank.

"What's going on?" said Ju. "And where's the koala?"

The girl kept on running and didn't look back in the direction of the hunters. Ju noticed that she'd dropped the larger stone but kept her grip on the flat one.

"The others don't want her anymore, do they?" said Ju, half to herself, half to the gobetween. "She's making a kind of knife or ax head, so that she can cut her own meat. But what has she done wrong?"

Ju remembered her ideas when she began the story. "What if the huntress didn't want to kill the koala? What would the tribe do?" She realized that she was still in control. The story had been following her thoughts until she picked up the narrative again. But where was the koala?

In answer, there was a rustling in a eucalyptus tree ahead of the girl. Ju made out a heavy gray shape propped in the fork where two thick branches met. Using his fingers, the animal was pulling branches toward him and tearing off the leaves with his teeth. His movements were rapid, yet at the same time nonchalant.

He paused midmouthful, leaves sprouting from his lips, and looked at the girl from the corner of his eye. She stopped running and raised her spear, as she had done before. This time there was no hesitation.

"Stop!" It was enough for Ju to think this for the girl to lower the weapon, though she kept her eyes fixed on the koala.

"It's no good her killing him—he's the only friend she has. They need to cooperate, not fight. Anyway, I'm sure there must be better things to eat."

Spreading his long fingers over the branch, the koala swung himself over the edge and hung there before plopping to the ground.

The girl bent over to put down the spear and the stone before picking up the koala. Though she was strong, she grunted as she lifted him to her shoulders. The koala climbed onto her back. He looked around him, chewing the rest of the leaves in his mouth.

"Outlaws," said Ju. "The tribe has rejected her, she spared his life, and now they depend on each other for survival." She felt a pang of fear, imagining herself in the girl's place. Would she manage to hunt and butcher a carcass without the rest of the tribe? Would the koala really be able to help her?

"Hmm." A lot to think about, and Ju remembered that she had work to do. "Gobey," she said, "that's enough for today."

While the girl froze, the koala jumped to the ground and loped toward Ju, just as he had done before. About to send him away, she was nevertheless curious. "What age is this?" she asked, forgetting that she did not want the koala to speak.

The koala stood on his hind legs. "Lower paleolithic," he said. "About four hundred thousand years ago. Before my time."

"Where is it? Australia?"

"No, I don't belong here. We're somewhere in southeast England. Kent."

Ju laughed. This was not the exotic setting that she had meant to conjure up. Still, nearly half a million years was a long way from home.

"Is she human?"

"Hominid," said the koala. "Some say she's a branch of *Homo sapiens,* of which you are one. But I wouldn't boast about her if she was my relative."

"How do you know all this?" said Ju.

"I have access to the entire gobetween," said the koala, opening his arms wide. "Wouldn't you like me for a companion?"

"I don't need companionship," said Ju. "I have plenty of friends."

The koala folded his short arms across his chest and eyed her beadily. "Are they able to offer information twenty-four hours of the day, give advice on any subject and answer you honestly when you ask for an opinion?"

He sounded self-assured, yet there was a hint of uncertainty in his voice that endeared him to Ju.

"What do I have to do?" she said.

The animat dropped his arms. "Tell your gobetween to make a transaction—that's all it takes."

"Money!" Ju exclaimed.

The koala looked pained. "Naturally. You cannot expect to have my services for free. The price is very competitive, I must say."

"No, thanks," said Ju. She felt cross. No wonder the koala was so talkative. He was programmed to give her a sales pitch. "Don't argue with me. Go away now."

He smiled coyly. "The customer is always right. I look forward to more of your story." He disappeared with the rest of the scene.

CHAPTER 31

It was time to lower the roof. Though it was far later in the day than intended, Mr. Bell was confident that the job could be completed. Gavin and Eager were allowed to climb the scaffolding of an outbuilding for a good view.

The sun was setting when the four cranes began to haul the roof into the air. Their profiles turned black against the orange backdrop.

"Do you know what I'm thinking?" said Gavin. Eager did not know, since he was not in the habit of reading people's thoughts. He understood it to be a rhetorical question and waited for his friend to continue.

"Those cranes are like priests of long ago, raising a huge stone into the air as an offering to the dying sun."

"Why would they do that?" said Eager.

Gavin shrugged. "Perhaps to appease the sun, if they thought it was angry with them. Or to persuade it to return the next morning. Imagine going to bed every night in fear that the sun might not rise. Life on this planet would stop if the sun disappeared."

"Would it stop for me and the other robots?" said Eager.

"Interesting question," said Gavin. "You don't rely on any of the life processes that the sun provides. But you need radio waves to power you, and they would fizzle out eventually."

Eager considered this scenario. "And no humans, or animals, or trees."

"No plants or any form of life. Some fish could survive, of course, though without the sun their food might die out. But the oceans would freeze in the end."

"Humans are very brave," said Eager.

"Why do you say that?"

"They live in mystery. You see, I know all about my origins and why I'm here. Professor Ogden built me to be like him, and to live and work with humans. But people don't know their purpose. They have to work it out for themselves."

Gavin was standing very close to him, and despite the fading light Eager could see the intensity of his gaze. "You've become very wise, Eager."

The robot was taken aback. Over the last few days, he'd been feeling anything but wise.

"Look!" Gavin cried, springing forward and pointing beyond the scaffolding. "The roof is over the building. They must be ready to lower it."

Eager thought about Jonquil and hoped that he was still

checking the operation. Eager could not be sure that he would not be distracted. His nephew was, after all, a very young robot.

"It's all right, Uncle Eager," said a familiar voice in his thoughts. "The calculations are exact this time. I'm on top of the crane. I'm going to be the first robot on the roof!"

Eager stepped forward to join Gavin. Together they looked across to the learning center. The four cranes stood one at each corner, like specters in the dusk. Between them, they supported the glassy sheet of the roof as it hung above the building.

In concert, the cranes began to lower the roof toward the carbon nanotubes. The downward movement was so gradual that it was hard to tell when it had finished. But before long, the cranes were sliding backward, revealing long forks that had held the roof.

Eager felt a moment's anxiety as the roof dropped, imperceptibly, onto its invisible pillars. There was no further movement.

"It's worked!" Gavin shouted. "Well done, Dad!" His voice was loud enough for Mr. Bell to have heard. From other parts of the building site came cheers and applause.

Gavin and Eager were about to climb down the scaffolding when light flooded the building opposite. They were able to see the space between the roof and the walls clearly. Although the roof must have been firmly in place, it appeared to be hovering above the building.

"It looks as if it might float away in the breeze," said Gavin.

"And yet we know how heavy it is!" He scrambled down the scaffolding, but Eager stayed a moment longer, admiring the beauty of the glass glowing in the light. Though the roof was not floating away, something on it was fluttering in the breeze— a golden flag.

CHAPTER 32

Gavin stretched out his long legs and leant back on the sofa in his parents' living room. He and his father had just finished telling Mrs. Bell the drama of the roof.

"Eager saved the day," Gavin said. "Not for the first time."

Eager shook his head. "I didn't do anything, really." Quite true.

"I'm glad I didn't know what was going on. I would have worried all day," said Mrs. Bell. "The thought of that roof crashing down . . ."

"And my career with it," said Mr. Bell gloomily.

"Come on, Dad," said Gavin. "Mistakes happen. The important thing is to spot them."

"That's just it—none of us noticed the error," said Mr. Bell. "If it hadn't been for Eager, we'd have gone ahead as planned. Professor Ogden is right. If we're going to rely on machines, we need truly intelligent ones."

"Like Eager," said Mrs. Bell, smiling at the robot.

"Thank you again," said Mr. Bell.

Eager lowered his head modestly. "Jonquil?" he said. "Were you listening? Mr. Bell was really thanking you, though he didn't know it. You saved his career."

Jonquil's voice came to him from under the coffee table. "I heard. I did today what I was designed to do. Isn't that right, Uncle Eager?"

"Yes!" said Eager.

The Bells were now talking about Molly.

"The International Space Authority?" Mrs. Bell was saying. "Does she know Sam?"

"I asked her, and she said no. But then, Molly's a biologist and he's an engineer," said Gavin.

"Where is she from?" continued Mrs. Bell. "She said she had only recently moved."

"Do you know"—Gavin laughed—"I don't know her nationality. She seems to have lived all over the world."

"Well, where do her parents live?"

"I don't know, Mum," said Gavin. "But she often talks about them, and about her grandparents too."

Mrs. Bell offered Gavin more tea. "Did you like Molly, Eager?" she said.

"Yes," said Eager. He tilted his head. "Have I seen her before? There is something about her face that recalls another facial pattern I once saw."

"She looks a bit like Tina, another friend of Gavin's," said

175

Mrs. Bell. For some reason, she glanced nervously at Gavin as she said this. "Perhaps you're thinking of Tina."

There was a discreet chime from Gavin's jinn. "Gavin, you have a call from Fleur."

"Hello," said Gavin. "You look happy."

"Sam's back at the moon base," said Fleur's voice. "I was so relieved to hear from him. He was tired, so he said he'd call again after a sleep. I thought it would be fun to have people round this evening, since he missed the get-together on Friday. Can you come? And would you like to bring Molly?"

"Thanks, I'll ask her," said Gavin.

"I'm going to call Mum and Dad. . . ."

Gavin grinned at his parents. "I'm with them now," he said. "But they said they wanted an early night. . . ." He looked at Mr. and Mrs. Bell, who nodded. "Dad's had a busy day. I'll tell you about it later. See you soon."

As Eager stood up to say goodbye to Gavin, something tugged at his leg, causing him to stumble. He looked down. A straw-colored rope had tied his ankle to the leg of the table.

"Are you all right?" said Mr. Bell.

"Take me too," said the rope.

"I'm not going anywhere," said Eager.

"That's good," said Mr. Bell. "I thought you were heading for the fruitcake just then."

"Can't we go too?" said Jonquil.

"We haven't been invited," explained Eager, in his thoughts.

But that very moment Gavin said, "Why don't you come, Eager? You won't have much opportunity to see Fleur otherwise. I'll put you in a pod to come back."

"Don't worry about us," said Mrs. Bell. "Gavin was right, we're off to bed."

As they walked along Wynston Avenue, Gavin called Molly and arranged to meet her at Fleur's house. He became pensive.

"Eager," he said at last, "I'm still puzzled how you spotted that error at the building site."

Eager tried to sound offhand. "You know that I can tune in to different robot frequencies. Sometimes it happens with the gobetween too."

"I see," said Gavin. "I remember that you used to speak with Sphere in your thoughts. That's the same sort of thing, I suppose."

They turned onto the main road.

"It's curious," Gavin went on. "I haven't seen Sphere for years, though I often spotted it when you lived with us. But whenever I see anything glowing that I can't explain at first, I think it must be a sunlike ball. Once I even called out, 'Sphere!' But it never is."

"I don't see Sphere often," said Eager. "Sometimes in the compound, when I'm feeling stuck over a problem, or . . ." He broke off. "Or when I miss being out in the world."

"What does it say to you?" said Gavin.

"It's more a feeling," said Eager. "A feeling that everything is all right, whatever is happening."

They heard the hum of the hoverbus and hurried to the stop.

"Well, things are certainly all right tonight," said Gavin as they climbed onto the bus. "Let's go and celebrate with Fleur and Ju."

"Hooray," said Jonquil's voice. "A party."

CHAPTER 33

Marcia and Finbar were the first to arrive at Fleur's house. The nurse greeted them with many curtsies. She seemed to think Marcia was a very important person.

Finbar held back in the hallway to talk to Ju.

"I'm really sorry," Ju said before he could speak. "I can't ask Dad's advice now that everyone's coming."

"It's all right. I thought it was a long shot anyway, so I told Mum on the way here," said Finbar.

"About the boy?" said Ju. Marcia had arrived laughing and smiling, not at all like someone who has just learned that she's been robbed.

"She took it very well," said Finbar. "In fact, she confessed that my choice in clothes was worrying her. She said turquoise is not my color!"

"What's she going to do?"

"Speak to her bank before going to the police, to see if they can trace the thief. She said it happens to lots of people."

"What about the boy impersonating you?" said Ju.

Finbar made a face. "I didn't tell her that bit. I don't know why. . . . I've got funny feelings about it. I thought I'd wait until she finds out more; then I'll decide what to do."

"Make haste! Make haste!" said the nurse, coming down the hallway.

"Well done," Ju said to Finbar. "I know you weren't looking forward to telling her."

The front door opened to let in the new arrivals. Everyone crowded into the living area. Gavin and Molly sat on the sofa; Marcia and Fleur took a chair each. Ju pulled back the partition to let Finbar and Eager perch on her bed.

"What shall we say when Sam calls?" said Marcia. "I feel we should sing something, like 'Happy Birthday.' "

"I think the sight of you all will be surprise enough. He won't have seen this many people in one room for weeks," said Fleur.

The smell of freshly baked pastry wafted into the room, followed by the nurse, bearing drinks and a plate of pies. "So this is the famous nurse," said Gavin, accepting a pie from the animat. "I hear you're a wonderful cook, Nurse." He winked at her.

"Why, you saucy knave! Enough of your ropery!" She turned on her heels and went back to the kitchen.

"Sam is here," said the gobetween.

"Wait!" cried Ju, grabbing a pastry and throwing herself down on a cushion.

Her father smiled out from the screen. He looked relaxed in

an open-neck shirt. The lucky stone was around his neck. His smile faltered. "What's going on?"

"Surprise!" said Fleur. She added anxiously, "Are you still feeling tired? Didn't you sleep?"

"I feel wonderful. Hello, everyone," said Sam, eyeing the visitors in the room. "I was taken aback for a moment."

"Since you missed the evening at Mum and Dad's, I thought you'd like to see everyone tonight. But if you're not feeling well . . ."

"Look at me, nine hours' beauty sleep." He showed his profile, then faced out again. "How are you all?" He scanned the room as if uncertain who to speak to first. "Who made those scrumdelicious pies?"

"Nurse," said Ju.

"Who?"

Ju laughed. "You don't know what's happened." She began to recount the events after the play. "All because Marcia told the director my real name was Juliet . . ."

"So you didn't all go to the theater?" said Sam, scanning their faces once more.

Marcia said, "I'm sorry again, Ju, if I embarrassed you."

Sam's eyes fixed on her. "Hello, Marcia. Fleur told me you'd arrived unexpectedly. Are you here for a holiday?"

"Mainly," said Marcia. "I'm taking Finbar to visit his grandparents, and we're going to Amsterdam, where I've a new exhibition."

"Are you enjoying yourself, Finbar?" said Sam, turning his attention to the corner of the room.

"Yes, thank you," said Finbar. "I'm not very used to cities, though."

Sam laughed. "Neither am I, anymore."

Gavin said, "Sam, can I introduce you to Molly? She works for ISA. . . ."

Sam looked at Gavin, and then at Molly beside him. "Hello, Molly. You're an astrobiologist, aren't you?"

Molly looked surprised. "Yes, I am, but I didn't think we'd met."

"I recognize your name, for some reason," said Sam with a smile. His expression changed. "Do you know, I am feeling tired. Perhaps I need to rest after all. Would you excuse me?"

"We want to hear about your trip," said Ju, disappointed.

Eager felt a violent pummeling across his shoulders. "What is it, Jonquil?" he thought.

"Uncle Eager, that isn't a human."

Eager was so shocked that he moved round to the side of the bed, where no one could see his face.

"I went into the gobetween's circuitry," said Jonquil. "I know the patterns it makes when there is a human on the screen. This is not a human, not like the people here."

"But what is he?" thought Eager. "An animat?"

"No. The nurse is an animat. The man on the screen is not like her."

"Then what?" thought Eager, glancing over his shoulder. The

noise level in the room had risen as everyone said goodbye to Sam.

"A simulation," said Jonquil.

Eager tilted his head. The enormity of the information was too much for him. A simulation!

"Yes," said Jonquil. "Computer-generated, like the Jones family."

Eager returned to his place beside Finbar. He heard Ju say dejectedly, "Bye then, Dad."

No one spoke as Sam's face ebbed from the screen.

"I'm sorry," said Fleur. "That wasn't as successful as I'd hoped. I thought we might hear about his trip."

Marcia said, "It must be a strain to be plunged into life on Earth all of a sudden."

Eager said to Gavin, in a low voice, "Can I talk to you?"

They went into the kitchen, where the nurse was clearing up.

"Nurse, will you leave us?" said Gavin. After she was gone, Eager said, "I saw into the gobetween just now, like I did at the building site today." He repeated what Jonquil had told him.

Gavin sat down, shocked.

"Can you have made a mistake, Jonquil?" said Eager in his thoughts.

"Do I make mistakes?" said Jonquil, who was still across his shoulders.

Eager considered this. His nephew often got into scrapes, but he had never failed in his work. "No," thought Eager glumly.

Gavin murmured, "It's incredible, but it makes sense. Sam's

behavior was so odd just now." He put his head in his hands. "How am I going to tell everyone, Eager?"

It was so like Gavin to take responsibility for Eager's bad news. The robot felt a surge of affection for his old friend. He had a sudden flash of understanding: if Molly was Gavin's special friend, she must feel a kind of affection for him too. Whatever the circumstances, Molly would be there to help Gavin.

CHAPTER 34

Gavin and Eager went back to the laughter and lively conversation. The nurse was saying, "Well, you have a fine husband, lady. Though his face be better than any man's, yet his leg exceeds all men's. . . ."

"That's enough!" Fleur giggled like a young girl.

Eager sat down on the bed. Gavin stood by the wall and asked for silence. Then he dropped his bombshell.

Ju burst into tears. To Eager's surprise, Fleur did not crumple as he had seen her do before when she received bad news. She simply stared at Gavin.

"I couldn't believe it at first," said Gavin. "But it was strange that he didn't greet me."

For a second no one spoke. Then everyone clamored to speak at once.

"I don't think he recognized me at all!" Marcia exclaimed. "It wasn't until Ju said my name that he spoke to me."

"He waited until my name was mentioned before talking to *me*," said Finbar.

"Whereas it's curious that he said he knew me, when we've never met," Molly said.

Ju wiped away her tears. "The conversation this afternoon was strange too. He didn't know what Mum meant when she said he'd taken off his lucky stone. And he said he wanted to chat, but then he said he was too tired!"

Molly nodded. "Perhaps the simulated Sam didn't have enough information to discuss things."

"Have you all gone mad?" said Fleur. "Why on earth would anyone make an expensive animat of my husband?"

"Not an animat," said Gavin, "a computer simulation."

Fleur shook her head. "I don't believe it. And since when did Eager have these powers?" Her voice rose. "And where's the real Sam? Tell me that!"

"Fleur," said Molly gently. "If the robot is right, I have an idea what might have happened."

"You know where Dad is?" cried Ju.

"No, but I think he's safe," Molly said.

"This is all nonsense!" Fleur stared angrily at Molly.

"At least hear Molly out," said Gavin, sitting next to her. She smiled gratefully at him.

"I shouldn't be telling you this," Molly said, "but I can't leave you to worry. Remember I talked about extraterrestrials the other night?"

Ju shrieked, "You're not saying Dad's been kidnapped by aliens?"

"No, no," soothed Molly. "That's science fiction. But you

said your father went to the listening station this weekend. As you know, there's a radio telescope there, searching for signals from intelligent life on other planets."

"Why did he go there?" asked Marcia. "Is that part of his job?"

Fleur shook her head. "He volunteered to take a new team of radio astronomers there. He was going to stay overnight and then bring back the old crew to the moon base. He went before and said he experienced the deepest peace ever, as if time had been suspended." She sounded as if she was holding back tears.

"That side of the moon never faces the earth, so there's no interference from terrestrial radio waves," said Molly. "That's why the far side is ideal for a listening station."

"And you think something happened at the station?" prompted Gavin.

Molly continued: "About a fortnight ago, there was a rumor that a strange signal had been picked up. The space community is buzzing with it. . . ."

"Why haven't the rest of us heard?" said Fleur. "The gobey tells me all the news about space."

"It's only a rumor," repeated Molly. "The International Space Authority would never let the public have that kind of information. They don't know what panic it might cause."

"What has this got to do with Sam?" demanded Fleur.

"If he was there when another signal was received, he would immediately become a security risk. ISA would take him to a safe place and debrief him," said Molly.

"Debrief him?" said Ju.

"Talk with him, to find out exactly what he had witnessed. In the meantime, ISA wouldn't want to worry you, nor could they tell you the truth. So they created a simulation, based on Sam's conversations with you over the years, and things like lists of people he's worked with or might have met—which may explain why he said he recognized my name."

"This is incredible," said Fleur.

"But compelling," said Marcia. "I can believe it of ISA. It's more secret than any Department of Defense. They wouldn't care about one man if they decided to hoodwink the world."

"Hoodwink the world?" said Gavin.

"Isn't that what they're doing?" said Marcia. "Keeping the truth from us, that there may be intelligent life out there?"

"For our own safety!" exclaimed Molly. "Who knows how people would react? In the twentieth century there were false reports of extraterrestrials, and people became frenzied! ISA is only waiting to be certain, and to decide how to tell everyone."

Marcia shrugged. "I think we can make up our own minds. It's the same with intelligent robots. . . ." She realized that she had said too much, and fell silent.

"So what do I do now?" said Fleur in a faint voice.

"Just wait," said Molly. "As soon as they've checked the signal—and it's probably another false alarm—they'll send Sam home. He'll still be considered a security risk if he goes back to work."

Ju's heart jumped. Some good might come out of the terrible situation, if her dad came home early!

"I can't wait," said Fleur firmly. "I need to know the truth."

Gavin leant toward her. "Fleur, we may have overlooked something." He half-turned to Molly. "It's possible, isn't it, that Sam understands the risks and is happy to be debriefed? He may even have helped ISA prepare the simulation."

"How can you suggest such a thing?" Fleur cried. "Have you no idea— "

"Fleur!" snapped Marcia. "Gavin's only trying to help. It's a sensible suggestion."

Fleur bit her lip. She took a deep breath. "I'm sorry, Gavin. But I know that Sam would never worry us like this. He would have said that a simulation was too chancy. And he'd be right, because it hasn't worked, has it?"

"It might have done if we hadn't all been here," said Molly. "The computer was thrown by the strange faces. Since you've never arranged a party before, ISA was unprepared for it."

Fleur shook her head. "Sam can't have helped them. He would never forget a detail like his lucky stone. He never takes it off." She said resolutely, "I'm going to tell ISA that I've guessed what's happened, and that I want to speak to Sam."

"You can try!" said Molly, a hint of scorn in her voice.

Fleur frowned. "What do you mean?"

"How can you prove what's happened?" said Molly. "Are you going to take Eager as a witness? Of course not. And if you try to tell people, ISA will simply wheel out Sam, looking perfectly normal, and have him say that nothing's wrong."

"The simulated Sam, you mean," said Gavin.

Molly nodded. "The power is in their hands."

"There must be something we can do," cried Fleur.

Molly looked uncertainly at her. "Perhaps there is," she said. "But it's more extraordinary than you can imagine."

CHAPTER 35

Early the next morning Eager took Jonquil on a walk around the neighborhood. They went as far as the old technocrats' quarter. The large eccentric houses had been built exclusively for technocrats and government officials; now they belonged to anyone who could afford them. The expanses of green that Eager remembered had disappeared under rows of new houses.

His nephew was enjoying the freedom of being outdoors. He hopped and rolled on the grass, changing from a ball to a paper-thin sheet and back again. Few people were out at that hour, but if Jonquil detected someone he instantly blended with his surroundings. Eager lost track of where he was and waited for the next eruption of grass to find out.

"Marcia used to live here," he said on one of Jonquil's re-appearances. "Up there, behind those trees."

"Why doesn't she live there now?" said Jonquil.

"Her parents moved away when they retired. But Marcia had

left home long before. Mrs. Bell said she quarreled with them, especially over the Ban."

"Why?"

"Her parents wanted it to be introduced, because robots had threatened them. But Marcia came to know me, and she said the new law was cruel and unnecessary."

"She said that?"

"Exactly that," said Eager.

Jonquil was silent for a second. "Why would humans make a law that was cruel and unnecessary?"

"I don't know," said Eager. "Only some people wanted it, but they were enough." He was touched that Jonquil should ask about his friends. He said, "How are the Joneses?"

Jonquil bounced in the air twice before replying, "I don't know."

"Yesterday was a busy day, I suppose," said Eager, "but don't you go to see them at night?"

Jonquil made another bounce. "Not anymore. Nothing happens."

"Nothing happens?" exclaimed Eager. "Something always happens to the Jones family, you told me so."

"Not to them—to me," said Jonquil.

Eager was puzzled.

"Whether Lori gets run over or runs away or runs a bath, it makes no difference to me. But when things happen to the Bells and their friends, I feel something." Jonquil hopped onto a nearby post and balanced there. "Haven't you been trying to tell me this, Uncle Eager?" Without waiting for a reply, he added, "Shall I show you? The Jones family is like this—" He became a square sheet, his fibers stretched so thinly that he was transparent. He tipped from one corner to another, and from every angle the square looked the same.

"And this is what real humans are like—" The square took off from the post, disappearing in a kaleidoscope of color.

The swirling mass tantalized Eager with different shapes; Jonquil's edges were messy, hard to define, constantly changing.

"Yes, that's life!" cried Eager, dazzled. He was relieved when Jonquil reverted to a straw-colored ball. Thinking of Fleur and her missing husband, he said, "Sometimes people might prefer a nice square piece of life."

"But it's flat, Uncle Eager!" cried Jonquil. "I don't want to live in Flatland. I want my life to be—" He was back to his shape-shifting and color-changing.

"Please stop," said Eager. "I don't want to live in Flatland either, but there is more than enough excitement for me at the moment."

"All right," said Jonquil, performing a starburst and settling on Eager's shoulders. "Shall we go back and see what's happening?"

CHAPTER 36

On the way to the Bells' house, Eager wondered whether Molly could really think of a plan to help Fleur and Ju. She had refused to be drawn the previous night, saying that it was only an idea and she would have to think about it.

"What's going to happen now?" said Jonquil, reading Eager's thoughts.

"We won't know until we hear from Gavin," said Eager.

They didn't have long to wait: Gavin and Molly were drinking coffee with Mr. and Mrs. Bell. Eager could tell they'd been told about Sam.

"Poor you," said Mrs. Bell, on seeing Eager. "It must have been a shock to discover the simulation."

"Yes!" said Eager.

"We've been to see Fleur and she's calmed down," said Gavin. "She said she understands what we're up against. But she wants to be certain that Sam is alive and well."

Molly said wearily, "I've been racking my brain trying to think how I might get that information—who I could ask. But

I know how tight security is at ISA. I'm too junior, I'd never get past it."

"Which is why we're here," said Gavin.

Eager noticed that all eyes were upon him.

"Why is everyone looking at you like that?" said Jonquil.

"I wish I knew," thought Eager.

"You see," Molly began, "I can't crack the security, but you can. If you can pick up signals from Fleur's gobetween, and the one at the building site, so Gavin tells me, then you can access the machines at the Space Authority."

"I can?" said Eager.

"*I* can," said Jonquil's voice in his ear.

"That's probably the easy bit," said Molly with a laugh. "The hardest bit is to get you inside ISA headquarters." She paused. "I've come to the conclusion that only boldness will work."

"What sort of boldness?" said Eager.

Molly's laugh was less comfortable this time. "Well, yours, really! But I was referring to the boldness of my plan."

"It certainly is a bold one," said Mr. Bell. "They're often the best."

"They're sounding like the Jones family," grumbled Jonquil. "Why don't they get on with it? What is this plan?"

"What is the plan?" asked Eager politely.

"No one can enter ISA who doesn't work there," said Molly. "The public can visit the space center nearby, but that's no use to us. And it's impossible to break into ISA. So, I asked myself, 'What would make ISA open its doors to you?' "

"What?" Eager could tell by her tone that she had an answer.

"The one thing that's on their mind—extraterrestrials."

Eager tilted his head. "Do we know any?"

Everyone laughed. "No one has ever met one," said Gavin, "which makes it easier for us to pretend that you're one."

It took Eager a moment to unravel Gavin's words. "That I'm an extraterrestrial?" he exclaimed.

"That's right," said Molly. "We shall have to cook up some story about how you came to be at ISA, but they're bound to take you for investigation."

Eager did not like the sound of this. "What exactly will they investigate?"

"People will ask you lots of questions. It could go on for days, but that won't matter. As soon as you've accessed the information we need, you'll be out of there."

"I will?"

Molly's eyes were shining as she leant toward him. "Yes, because I'll have returned to work by then, and I can help you escape. Believe me, it's a lot easier to get out of there than in."

Gavin's face was glowing too. "Bold, but stunningly simple."

"What's the catch?" said Jonquil in Eager's ear.

"Pardon?" thought Eager.

"If something sounds that good, there's always a catch. That's what Mr. Jones says."

Eager didn't want to take advice from Mr. Jones, who not only sounded a miserable person but was not even a person at all. However, Eager had qualms of his own.

"I arrive at the International Space Authority headquarters and tell them I'm from another planet, and while they're investigating me with lots of questions, I find out where Sam is, and then I leave?" he said.

"In a nutshell," said Gavin.

"But . . ." Eager hesitated. He was unsure how to say this in front of Molly, who did not know that he was in hiding because of the Ban. "I lived in the world a long time. Other people—technocrats—have met me. What if someone recognizes me?"

Mr. and Mrs. Bell gave little nods to each other. Their faces were drawn.

"Mum and Dad pointed this out," said Gavin. "But that was years ago. The people who work for ISA are different sorts of scientists, mostly."

Molly said slowly, "In a way, it doesn't matter if someone raises a suspicion about you. ISA will still have to investigate, and that's all we need."

Gavin nodded. "The upshot is, if they've never seen a robot like you before, and you turn up on the doorstep—even if you said you were a milkman, they'd probably be interested."

"And if you say you're an alien, they're bound to be," said Molly. "They're taking these signals from space very seriously."

"It's still a big risk for Eager," said Mr. Bell. "I know you want to help Fleur," he said to the robot, "but you must think of your own safety."

"I'll go!" said Eager at the mention of Fleur's name. "We all want to know that Sam is safe. And if Molly can get me out again, I've nothing to be worried about."

There were smiles all round, though those of Mr. and Mrs. Bell were more hesitant.

Eager's mind was full of thoughts. For some days he'd managed to cover for his nephew, but how much longer could he keep it up? "I think I should tell them about you," he said in his mind to Jonquil.

"Whatever you say, Uncle Eager."

Eager was about to speak when the words came into his head: "Don't tell Molly." He closed his mouth and tilted his head to one side while he reasoned with himself. Molly must have some idea what sort of robot he was, to entrust him with her plan. But Jonquil was a different matter: Professor Ogden had called him "world-shattering." It would be a risk to tell Molly about Jonquil. On the other hand, she was Gavin's special friend and she was putting herself in danger to help the Bells.

"Eager," said Molly, pulling her chair closer to where he was standing. "I want you to know, I would never harm you, or allow harm to come to you. I've promised Gavin that. He wouldn't have let me come here, otherwise." She smiled shyly at Gavin over her shoulder.

This decided Eager. He opened his mouth a second time.

"Don't tell Molly!" The words were crystal clear, as if Sphere, the luminous ball, had spoken them to him. But when Eager looked rapidly about him, there was no sign of Sphere. "Did you speak to me, Jonquil?" he thought.

"No."

Gavin coughed. "Eager, I'm sorry to hurry you. If you're having second thoughts . . ."

"No," said Eager. "I'll go."

"I'm coming too?" said Jonquil's voice, a little unsure.

"Of course," thought Eager. "We need you."

CHAPTER 37

Gavin and Molly intended to leave immediately. "Good thing robots don't have to pack," said Mrs. Bell.

"I'm due back at work tomorrow," explained Molly. "If we catch a train now, Eager can be at ISA by tonight."

"Where is ISA?" said Eager. It sounded like a long journey.

"France," said Mr. Bell.

Gavin had hired a flying pod, which was waiting in the road. Mr. and Mrs. Bell stood under the lime tree to wave them off.

"Don't forget," said Mr. Bell as the robot climbed into the backseat, "there is such a thing as being too brave. Remember that Molly will be there to help you."

The pod rose into the air. Eager looked down at the avenue, the lime tree, the receding figures of Mr. and Mrs. Bell, and wondered how long before he would return. Would he miss the rest of his week there? The thought reminded him of Allegra. As far as she was concerned, Jonquil was already a long way from home. What would she say if she knew that Eager was taking him abroad!

Molly's voice interrupted his thoughts. "We have to go to Fleur's house, to collect something."

Twenty minutes later, the flying pod swooped down in front of the dance school. Drumbeats resonated from the building as Eager followed Gavin and Molly into the lift.

"The thing is, a single alien doesn't make a delegation," said Gavin.

Eager realized that Gavin was speaking to him. "Is that a proverb?" he said.

Gavin laughed. "Not yet!" The lift door opened and they stepped onto the roof. "It means we need another alien," he said.

Before Eager could ask him what he meant, the nurse was greeting them at the door. "O, here you are! Make haste, make haste!" she cried. "My lady lies weeping, blubbering and weeping, weeping and blubbering!"

"Peace, Nurse!" cried Marcia from the hallway. "Ignore her," she told the visitors. "Of course Fleur and Ju are upset, so Finbar and I stayed the night. But it seems to have triggered something in the nurse." She led them into the living room, where Fleur joined them.

"We've got a suggestion," Fleur said without preamble. "Take Ju and Finbar."

"What?" said Gavin.

"They want to go, they've been pleading with us all morning," said Marcia. "It'll give you a reason for going, Gavin. If anyone asks, you're taking your niece and her friend on a trip to the space center, with a couple of robots to help you."

Gavin looked at Molly for guidance.

Fleur said, "Marcia's managed to convince me they won't be in any danger—"

"How can they be?" interrupted Marcia. "They won't go to ISA, just the space center, like any other tourists."

"I'm worried that Ju will fret if she stays," said Fleur. "At least the trip will make her feel she's doing something. I wish I could come for the same reason."

"But you have to stay for when 'Sam' calls. He mustn't suspect anything," said Marcia in a tone that suggested they had already had this conversation.

"How long will it take them to get ready?" Molly asked.

Marcia laughed. "I think you'll find they've already packed!"

Ju came into the room. "Well, can we?" she said, her eyes roving over the faces.

"You can," said Fleur.

"Will we be back by Friday? I'm meeting my friend Luisa in the evening," said Ju.

Molly nodded. "Eager should only need a day at ISA, so you can travel back on Thursday."

Ju turned tail and called for Finbar. "Grab your bag, we're going!"

Marcia said to Molly, "What tickets do we have to buy for the children . . . ?"

Fleur took Gavin to one side. "Ju knows all about Eager," she whispered. "Marcia had already told Finbar, so I decided to tell

Ju. She understands. She'll keep it secret." Finbar appeared with a small pack in his hand.

"Is that all?" said Gavin.

"Finbar travels light. He's not interested in clothes," said Marcia proudly. Finbar shot her a look of surprise. Whenever she had said this before, her tone had been despairing. Everyone, including the nurse, congregated in the hallway.

"Now, Nurse," said Fleur, indicating Gavin, "you must do what this gentleman says at all times."

"Yes, my lady," said the nurse.

Fleur turned to Eager and kissed him on the cheek. "Thank you," she said.

"I'll do my best," said Eager.

"I know you will," said Fleur. She turned away abruptly and embraced her daughter. Marcia hugged Finbar.

"Is that the other alien?" said Jonquil's voice as the nurse preceded them out of the house.

"I believe so," said Eager.

CHAPTER 38

The International Railway Terminus building was a huge glass igloo. Its inner workings—the offices, tracks, shops—and the dozens of people bustling or loitering outside them were all exposed to view.

"Does anyone need a ticket?" said Gavin.

Ju looked at her jinn. "No, Mum has just bought me one."

"Same here," said Finbar.

"Do robots need tickets?" said Eager.

"They certainly do. They're on my jinn with mine," said Gavin. "We can catch the next train." He looked at Molly. "Had we better split up?"

"Yes," said Molly. "I can't risk being seen with you now. But we'll need to meet later on the train so I can brief Eager and the nurse."

She hurried into the building. The others waited a minute before they followed. They crossed the concourse toward the platforms. Finbar spotted Molly in a shop, choosing a book to download on her lexiscreen. He quickly glanced away.

"Tickets," said the animat at the gate to the platforms. He was thin and balding. Ju wondered whether he had been designed at the whim of the manufacturers or was modeled on a real person. The ticket controller scanned Ju's and Finbar's jinns and passed on their seat numbers electronically. When he came to Gavin he paused. "You know the robots will have to sit with the baggage?"

"Baggage? Baggage?" cried the nurse, who appeared to take this as a personal insult. "Afore God, I am so vexed that every part of me quivers! You scurvy knave!"

The controller sat bolt upright as if ready to defend himself from attack.

"Peace, Nurse," said Ju. "You misunderstand."

"I was hoping we'd all sit together," said Gavin. "We're a party."

"I'm sorry, sir. These are the practices of the railway company. Now, if I may scan your jinn . . ."

"Is the train full?" Gavin persisted. "Surely the robots can join us if there are spaces?"

"I'm sorry," repeated the animat. "I can see that you are cross, sir. But I cannot change company policy."

"Uncle Eager, tell Gavin not to worry," said Jonquil's voice.

Before Eager could speak, Ju said anxiously, "Uncle Gavin, we shouldn't draw attention to ourselves, should we?"

"You're right." Gavin led the children and the robots away, checking his jinn as he did so. He exclaimed, "Looks like our seats are together after all!"

They joined the short queue for a retinogram. Finbar remembered waiting in line at the airport, when he had spotted the white-haired man. His thoughts turned to the boy on the Sorbjet. He felt happier now that Marcia was dealing with the theft, but he still had unfinished business with the nameless boy. . . .

It was his turn for a retinogram. He took Ju's place at the machine. Behind him Gavin was saying, "These robots are with me. I have their tickets."

"I need to scan the robots for their serial numbers and identification," said an official from behind a gobetween screen.

Eager shook his head at Gavin. He did not have a serial number, let alone a place to keep it in. The nurse stepped ahead of him and offered the palm of her hand to the man's scanner. The man read out her serial number from the scanner and checked it against information that appeared on the gobetween.

"Nurse, theatrical animat," he read. He eyed the nurse up and down. "You seem to fit the bill," he said. "On you go."

He turned his attention to Eager. The robot saw Gavin shrug helplessly.

"Show him your hand, Uncle Eager," said Jonquil.

Eager hesitated, but he had learnt by now to trust in his nephew's abilities. He held out his left hand, and the official passed his scanner over it.

"11497G," the man read. He glanced at the gobetween screen. "Sumo wrestler?" he said. He looked back at Eager, his expression darkening.

"Smile," said Jonquil.

Smile was the last thing Eager wanted to do, but he complied. It had no effect: the man was reaching for an emergency button on his desk. As he did so, his eye passed over the scanner screen. He did a double take. "11497K?" he said disbelievingly. He checked the number again. Glancing mistrustfully at Eager, he looked down at the gobetween.

The screen now read:

SURFY

DOMESTIC ROBOT

"Domestic robot—sounds more like it," the man said. He jerked his head at Eager. "Off you go, then, Surfy."

"How did you manage that?" said Finbar when Eager joined the others.

"There are ways," said Eager in an uncharacteristic mumble. He did not want to be asked any questions. There was no time, in any case, for Gavin was ushering them toward the platform. "Surfy!" thought Eager indignantly.

"I'm very sorry, Uncle Eager," said Jonquil. "I was trying to write 'surfysticated domestic robot,' because I know you're no ordinary robot. But I paused to think of the spelling, and the machine made me go to the next line."

"It's soph-isticated, not surf-ysticated," said Eager.

"Sorry," repeated Jonquil.

Eager took a final look at the terminus. Though it fascinated him, it also filled him with alarm. It was a very different public space from the theater, where everyone came to enjoy the spectacle. This was a place where the public itself was scrutinized and called to account.

The nurse, however, had grown calmer. She appeared to be at home among the officials and their prying machines. "She must be used to traveling," observed Gavin to the children as they approached the platform.

A sleek-nosed hovertrain waited, like a whippet about to race. It was then that the nurse lost her composure. "Fie! 'Tis a serpent! A monster of the sea!" she cried when Gavin invited her to climb inside.

"Think of it as a carriage, like the hovercar," said Ju, which was the wrong way to put it, she knew. The nurse obstinately refused to go aboard.

While Gavin remonstrated with her, the nurse's headdress slipped down her forehead and over her eyes. She put up her hands to right it, and Gavin and Finbar seized her by the elbows and bundled her onto the train. The unruly section of her headdress, meanwhile, had mysteriously disappeared.

"Now, my good woman," said Gavin when her sight had been restored, "pray take a seat," and he ushered her into the compartment.

"This is nice," said Ju, observing the plush striped seats with cushions. There were flowers on the table and a basket of fruit, wine and soft drinks.

"Odd," said Gavin. "We seem to be in first class." He sank down on one of the chairs. "Not only are we all together, but we've been upgraded too!"

"Thank you, Jonquil," said Eager silently.

"I only chose an empty compartment," said Jonquil. "Is first class good?"

The train let out a low hum as its engines started. It began to rise, which the passengers could tell only by looking out of the window at the adjacent train. Slowly, the train moved off on its invisible pillow of air. As they gained speed, the door of the compartment opened and Molly walked in. "My ticket says I'm in here!" she exclaimed.

Gavin grinned at her. "Sit down and have a drink," he said.

Eventually Molly left Gavin's side and took a seat opposite the nurse and Eager. "I need to tell you how to be an alien," she said.

Ju overheard. She leant across the aisle toward Molly. "You can't teach the nurse anything that isn't to do with the sixteenth century," she said. "That's all she's programmed to understand. My mum explained it to me."

"Don't worry," said Molly, smiling. "It isn't a problem. In fact, it's an asset. But I need to brief Eager; he'll have to do all the talking."

Ju sat back and turned on her lexiscreen. It made her dizzy to look out of the window as the countryside sped by at hundreds of kilometers an hour. Finbar was staring out, but she suspected that he was lost in thought rather than admiring the blurred view. She guessed, rightly, that he was thinking about the boy on the Sorbjet. Soon, tired after their late night, they both fell asleep.

Molly spent the journey talking to Eager, showing him maps and drawing him diagrams on a lexiscreen. Eager spared a thought for Sam, who was possibly being debriefed, which sounded like being briefed in reverse. He hoped the man was not drowning in information as he was. "I trust you're remembering all this," he said to Jonquil in his mind.

A few hours later, the hovertrain sailed slowly to its resting place. It was early evening, local time, yet the sun was still high. Inside the terminus—an older, darker building than the other—they went through immigration again. There was a chuckle as Eager's hand was scanned. With Jonquil's assistance, the same serial number and information appeared as before. Eager heard the officials chorusing, as he left the station:

"*Bonnes vacances,* Surfy!"

"So much for traveling incognito," said Gavin.

CHAPTER 39

"This is where I leave you," said Gavin, bringing the hired hovercar to a halt. He looked over his shoulder at the nurse and Eager. The three of them had been traveling for some time along a dusty road in the middle of the countryside. Molly had gone home to her apartment in the city, and Ju and Finbar had stayed behind at the hotel, to swim in the pool.

"We walk from here?" said Eager.

"Yes." Gavin glanced at a map on the dashboard that was illuminating the route they were on. "ISA's headquarters are a couple of kilometers along the main road over there. Molly thinks you should be stopped before you reach ISA. The road is heavily patrolled."

The back door opened and Eager swung his feet onto the ground. Gavin stretched out his arm and caught Eager's hand.

He squeezed it. "Good luck. Remember, this is not a question of life and death. Whatever you find out will reassure Fleur, but you can't alter things for Sam. So please, take care."

"I will, Gavin."

Gavin climbed out of the car to open the other door for the nurse. "It's time to pass the baton of command," he told Eager. "Now, my good woman, do as this gentleman tells you, at all times."

The nurse leant on his arm as she struggled to get out of the car. "Aye, sir, my lady Juliet told me the same, God bless her."

Gavin winked at Eager. "Now, whatever you do, don't say 'Take me to your leader'!" He got into the car and waved as he drove off.

Eager stood there, puzzled. "I always say 'please,' " he said. He and the nurse trudged along the track until it joined the main road, where they turned in the direction Gavin had indicated. Their going was slow, on account of the nurse's limp, but Eager was happy to absorb the scenery. The land was hilly and dotted with trees and rocks; the rocks appeared to be gray, though so did everything in the dusk.

"I think those are cypress trees," Eager said in his thoughts before he realized that he could talk openly now. It surprised him that Jonquil had not materialized to enjoy his freedom.

"Jonquil?" he said anxiously.

"Here I am." A bundle of fibers waved from the large pocket of the nurse's apron. Jonquil jumped out and shook himself mop-headedly. "It's very messy in there," he complained. "I found a wooden spoon, an apple core and a sock."

"You'd better return to my shoulders," said Eager. "The ground is very dusty."

A few meters on, they rounded a bend and saw a low building ahead of them. Two men were sitting at a table in front of the doorway. They each faced a small gobetween screen and seemed to be competing at something, for when one cheered, the other groaned. A carafe and two glasses stood next to the gobetweens.

Eager came closer. "I'm sorry to interrupt," he called.

The darker of the two men sprang to his feet. *"Halte! Qui êtes vous?"*

The nurse cried, *"Honi soit qui mal y pense!"* Eager shot her an admiring glance.

The man cried, *"Qu'est-ce que c'est?"*, pointing to the nurse's apron.

"I'm afraid I don't understand," said Eager.

"I saw something move," said the man in accented English. Jonquil!

"Empty your pocket, madame!"

The nurse became flustered. "Surfy!" she called to Eager.

Eager glared at her. Of course, she had never been introduced to him and had heard the name at the station. "Surfy, my fan!" cried the nurse. Eager looked at her in bewilderment. She thrust her hand into her apron pocket, pulling out an exquisite lace fan. She held the fan to her face and peeped coyly over the top of it at the men. "God ye good morrow, gentlemen," she said.

The man relaxed his stance. "Madame, I don't think you will shoot me with your fan," he said.

The guard still sitting at the table laughed. He was tall and sandy-haired. "Where are you from?" he called.

"Verona, sir," said the nurse promptly.

"Verona on Maoz," said Eager. "No doubt you know it as belonging to Alpha Centauri B."

The tall man grinned. "I don't think I know it as anything. Do you know it, Didier?"

"I don't think so," said his companion. "It's not around here."

"No," said Eager. "It's over four light-years away, which is . . ."

"Forty trillion kilometers," said the nurse's fan.

"Forty trillion kilometers," said Eager. "In Earth measurements, that is."

The tall man pushed back the peak of his cap. "That's a long way."

"We flew, of course," said Eager.

"Of course," murmured the man, sounding dazed.

"Henri!" said the other man. "Look at them! They're robots. The female is an animat, and this one . . . well, I would not like to say."

"They don't talk like any robots I have ever met," said Henri.

"Ils ont perdu la boule," said Didier.

"I beg your pardon?" Eager ventured to ask.

"You have lost your marbles," said Didier. "That's why some-one has left you here, in the middle of nowhere. Come, Henri, we should take them to the dump."

Eager's first reaction was to panic; then he remembered

214

Gavin's advice to be polite. "Excuse me, gentlemen. We're not looking for marbles, we're looking for the International Space Authority."

Didier's companion beckoned him to the doorway. They conferred.

"We have decided," said Didier.

"Yes," said Henri. "Everyone talks about extraterrestrials, but who really believes they will ever land? However, we will appear very stupid if you are the real thing and we have taken you to the dump. So we will deliver you to ISA."

"Let them decide what to do," said Didier.

"Thank you," said Eager.

CHAPTER 48

Ju sat cross-legged on the floor of the hotel's gobey-hall. It was a small room looked after by a young technician. He came and stood beside her.

"How can I help?" he asked.

"I'd like to call up something I'm working on at home," said Ju.

The man shrugged. "No problem. Tell the gobey the subject and your address, so that it can talk to your own gobetween."

When he had gone, Ju told the gobetween, "It's a story about a huntress and a koala."

While she waited, she reflected on Eager's mission. It seemed a crazy thing to do, to pretend to be an alien. On the other hand, who would ever have thought that ISA would make a simulation of her father? She hoped fervently that her dad was safe, and Eager too. "And even that silly old nurse," she thought.

The far screen was beginning to show images. They were dark and fleeting at first. Ju frowned, wondering whether she should call the technician. Then she realized that the play of shadow and light was part of the scene itself.

The girl and the koala were in a cave, curled up together beside the embers of a fire. A fur half-covered the girl, besides the fur she was wearing. This was new: she must have killed an animal and expertly skinned it. The koala sneezed in his sleep. The ear that was visible twitched. What was he dreaming about? Jungles of luscious eucalyptus trees? Ju was considering what she might cause to wake them, when the koala stirred. He lifted his head and opened one eye, looking out at Ju. The girl continued to sleep, her breathing heavy. Slipping from under her arm, the koala came to sit with his back to the fire.

"Hello," he half-growled. "Have you thought about my invitation?"

"To buy you?" said Ju.

The koala wrinkled his nose. He was looking particularly cute and the gesture made him more so. "I'm not a product in the supermarket. My companionship is for sale. Did you see me just now? Lying there, like a teddy bear?"

"I'm too old for teddy bears," said Ju. But the thought came to her: was anyone ever too old for a cuddly, comforting toy, especially if that toy could advise you?

"Tell me what I should do now," said Ju. "My dad has disappeared. We think he's being held by the authorities."

The koala blinked. Today his eyes seemed less beady and more like dark pools. "That's a terrible thing to happen," he said. "But there's nothing you can do."

"Nothing?" said Ju.

"The authorities are always right," said the koala.

"Are they?" said Ju in a tone that suggested she did not agree.

The koala seemed not to notice. "They are," he repeated. "But I shall take your mind off your worries. Accompany me on the gobetween and I'll introduce you to my friends."

Ju was unsure what to say. The gobeyhall door opened again. "Ju, are you still here?" came Finbar's voice.

She turned to him in the dark. "Yes, come on in."

He stopped halfway across the room, looking at the screen.

"It's just a story I'm telling," said Ju, suddenly embarrassed.

"That's fun," said Finbar. He stepped closer. "You know koalas don't look quite like that?"

"They don't?" said Ju, going back to the screen. "I've never seen one, but I asked the gobetween for a proper animal."

"I've seen lots of them," said Finbar. "Koalas this size are heavy, rather than cuddly. And they don't have much expression, whereas this one looks very alert. They're not as cute either, except when they're asleep."

"I see," said Ju. "It's funny . . . he looked real at first. I think he's been getting more teddy bear–like."

"Have you changed the story?"

"No," said Ju. "But he's based on an animat. He wants me to buy him."

"Expensive," said Finbar.

Ju nodded. "Do you think it's a sales tactic—making him more appealing to me?"

"I'm sure it is," said Finbar. "Some companies are very determined. A billscreen stopped me by the hotel when I first arrived, and would have grabbed me by the neck if it could."

She laughed. "Gobey, switch off. And don't let the koala argue with me." She turned to Finbar. "Do you want a go?" Though it was hard to tell in the dark, she fancied that he had a sheepish look.

"Well, I was wondering about returning to Amsterdam . . . ," he began.

"To the gallery?"

"No, I've been back already. The boy has signed my name in the visitors' book. I thought I'd see what else he's been up to."

"Do you want me to go?" said Ju.

"I'd like you to stay. I promise I'm not angry with him anymore." Finbar sat on the floor next to Ju. "Gobey, I want to see what's been happening in Amsterdam society."

"What sort of society?" said the gobetween.

"Good question," said Finbar. "The rich and famous."

The koala and the girl had disappeared, along with the cave. The screen now filled with a newsreel of glamorously dressed people, entering and exiting theaters and gobeyhalls, raising their glasses at parties and looking earnest at fund-raising events. In their wake was the boy from the Sorbjet, in a variety of vivid costumes.

"He looks so confident!" said Ju. "Is he really still pretending to be you?"

"Looks like it," said Finbar. There was no rancor in his voice. "As you can see, the turquoise suit wasn't his only purchase."

"But he isn't a bit like you. He's pale and pasty."

"What should Finbar Khan look like? It isn't an easy name to pin down," said Finbar with a smile in his voice.

Ju turned to him, trying to make out his expression. "You were right—you're not angry anymore."

"What's the point?" said Finbar. "I was cross because he cheated and deceived me. But I think the worst thing was feeling it was my fault. I should have known better. I don't usually trust people that quickly. . . ." He broke off, remembering that he had been reluctant to confide in Ju at first. "Anyway, it helps to know that the bank is dealing with the theft. Mum says the account has been set up differently so he can't access it again."

"But he's telling everyone he's you!"

Finbar shrugged. "I know. I'm going to have to think what to do." He stood up. "It's getting late. Gavin should be back and we can have dinner."

"Good, I'm starving," said Ju. She paused in the doorway. "Fancy thinking about food when Dad's missing."

"You won't help him by starving yourself," said Finbar. "Besides, Eager's on the case. I never thought I'd say this of a robot, but if anyone can pull this off, he can."

CHAPTER 41

Eager and the nurse sat in the back of an armored vehicle. They were as high above the ground as they had been in Gavin's hovercar, but the truck's wheels were firmly on the road. The scenery had not changed, though here and there a house appeared on a hilltop. It was growing dark. The nurse let her head drop, as though she was snoozing. She had put away her fan, and Jonquil stayed hidden in her pocket.

"Are you from this area?" said Eager conversationally.

"Originally," said Didier, who was the first to respond. He set the vehicle to drive itself and turned sideways in his seat to talk to the passengers. "I have traveled a lot. I worked on a cruise ship before I became a patrol guard. I speak nine languages."

"Yours must be a very important job," said Eager, "since it cannot be trusted to animats."

"Well, yes," said Didier. "Space, you know, has the highest of all security ratings."

Henri swiveled round. "I am not from here," he said. "But I love the region—the climate, the food. I love to cook."

"Ah, yes," said Eager, thinking of the times when he cooked for the Bells.

"Do you cook?" said Henri.

"No," said Eager hastily. "But my fellow Maozians, who are humanoid, they enjoy eating."

"So you are not all robots on Maoz?"

"Oh, no," said Eager. "I'm a product of humanoid technology. Naturally they had to send robots into space for such a long journey."

"Naturally," said Henri. "And what is the climate like on Maoz?"

"Mild," said Eager. They had reached a fence with a tower at the corner.

"Checkpoint One," said Didier. "Its sensors have recognized us and are letting us pass." They drove on, skirting the fence. Eager peered out and decided that it was a hot-fence, which would scorch anyone who tried to climb it. The barrier ended in a wide gate with a tower similar to the checkpoint's. Lights so powerful that they created a false dawn lit up the road and the tower.

The truck was obliged to stop in front of the closed gate. A soldier climbed down from the tower and walked up to Didier's window. He had a large florid face. "What brings you here? Is there a problem?"

Didier glanced nervously at Henri, who nodded encouragingly. "We've brought you some visitors," Didier said.

"Visitors?" said the man. "Are we having a party? Look over there." He jerked his thumb at a large sign of a man and a woman, scored through with a cross. "That sign means 'No unauthorized personnel.' If you press the button underneath you get it in fifty different languages, to be on the safe side."

Didier looked sourly at him. "I don't expect it is in Maozian," he said.

"Maozian?"

"That is what the visitors speak," said Didier. "They are from Maoz."

"Maoz!" roared the man. "Maoz, my ass!"

The patrol guards assumed pained expressions. "There is no need to be vulgar," said Didier.

Henri leant across to the window. He said, "If you don't want them, we will take them to the Department of Defense."

The soldier glowered at him. He appeared to be struggling with himself. "Wait here," he said, turning abruptly on his heels.

"That got him," said Henri gleefully as the soldier disappeared into the tower.

"Got him where?" said Eager.

"The Defense Department and ISA, they are always bickering," said Didier. "The Space Authority would not want the defense people to get the credit, if you are really extraterrestrials."

"They would have lots of egg on their faces," said Henri.

"Imagine, they are the Space Authority, and they did not recognize an alien when he arrived!"

The soldier had returned from the tower. "You can go in," he said in a surly voice. The gates opened and the truck crawled forward to deliver Eager and the nurse to the International Space Authority.

CHAPTER 42

Eager and the nurse said goodbye to Didier and Henri. As the truck turned round in the open quad, the soldier marched the robots into the building.

"In here," said the soldier, indicating a windowless room furnished with a desk, benches and chairs. Eager and the nurse sat on a bench together.

Before long, a woman with an unsmiling expression came into the room. She sat at the table and put down the lexiscreen that she was carrying. "I am Dr. Shu. I am here to ask you questions," she said.

"That would be the debriefing," said Eager enthusiastically.

The woman shot him a look, but her expression did not change. Eager noticed that there were shadows under her eyes, as if she had been up for a long time. Her eyes reminded him a little of Molly's. She took out a stylus from the lexiscreen. "I shall take down your answers myself."

"Good idea," said Eager.

The woman frowned. "I wouldn't try to ingratiate yourself with me," she said. "I am only here to ask questions. The decisions to be made about you are entirely out of my hands." She looked down at the lexiscreen.

"That must be a relief," said Eager.

"Pardon?" said the woman.

"Not to be the one to make the decisions," explained Eager.

"I certainly wouldn't want to decide whether *you* were an extraterrestrial or not."

The woman eyed him. "Can we begin?" she said. "Where are you from?"

"Verona, madam," said the nurse.

"Verona on Maoz," said Eager, who was well rehearsed by now. "It's a small planet just off Alpha Centauri B, which is—"

"I know where Alpha Centauri is!" said the woman. "Every schoolchild knows that it's the closest star system to us." She began to write. "So, your planet orbits the star Alpha Centauri."

"B," said Eager.

"B," repeated the woman. "And your name is?"

"Why, my lord is called Surfy," said the nurse. "Fie, do you not know him?"

The damage was done, but Eager saw a chance to soften the indignity. "Sir Fie," he said to the nurse. "That's my name. Remember it."

The woman paused, her stylus hovering above the lexiscreen. "Can we get this straight? Surfy, or Surfye?"

226

"Sir Fie," said Eager. "My friend confuses her Earthly pronunciation sometimes. It's spelt S-I-R F-I-E."

"An honorary title, I suppose," said the woman as she recorded it. "And your name?" she said to the nurse.

"Nurse," said the animat.

"She's our medical officer," said Eager, seeing the woman frown again.

"Medical officer?" The woman rolled the words on her tongue. "I suppose that's why she has such a clean apron," she said sarcastically.

Eager gave the woman a frosty look. "We've traveled a long way," he said.

The interrogator spent some time writing. She looked up at last. "It would appear that Maoz is a hierarchical society."

Eager was not sure what this meant. "Well," he mused, "we are certainly higher in terms of being technologically advanced. But I wouldn't say we were rarchical, would you, Nurse?"

"Nay, Sir Fic," said the nurse, "we are never rarchical, though I cannot say no to a dish of eels and a piece of marchpane." She winked at him.

The woman lowered her stylus. "Shall we move on? If you've come here from Maoz, where is your spaceship?"

"In orbit," said Eager. "We parachuted from there. The lack of oxygen is no problem for robots. Though it was a bit awkward for my companion in her skirt." He added, "That's why we haven't brought any gifts, I'm afraid. We are only the advance party."

The woman seemed to be having trouble writing. "And why did you come here?" she said.

"A friendly visit," said Eager. "We picked up a radio message from you, inviting us, about five hundred years ago—Earth years, that is. It's taken all that time to get here. Though as you know, space-time is a bit different," he added.

"Yes, I do know," said the woman. She wrote furiously for a while.

"It's going well." Eager sent the thought to Jonquil, who was across his shoulders. "Thanks to Molly's briefing, I'm enjoying this *de*briefing!"

The woman looked up. Her forehead was furrowed. "You say you received an invitation from Earth?"

"That's right," said Eager. "Very nicely expressed. It took us a while to decipher it, but we also received a pictorial dictionary and a phonetic guide. That's why the nurse is able to speak perfect sixteenth-century English, whereas I've studied present-day English from your gobetween transmissions. We pick them up by satellite. Have you ever watched *Stars in Space*?"

"Just wait a minute!" said the woman. "You say that you received a message from Earth, sent in the sixteenth century? It isn't possible."

"It isn't?" said Eager.

"Of course not! The technology wasn't available. It would have taken someone far ahead of their time to send a radio message into space. Someone of extraordinary vision and engineering ability! Who could possibly have done it?"

"Who?" thought Eager.

"I think Molly forgot to tell us," said Jonquil.

"Leonardo da Vinci!" exclaimed the nurse. "A man, Sir Fie . . . such a man as all the world . . . Nay, he's a flower; in faith, a very flower."

"Leonardo da Vinci . . . ?" murmured the woman.

"God be with his soul! An eagle, Sir Fie, had not so green, so quick, so fair an eye as Leonardo!"

"Nurse . . . ," said Eager.

"Nay, I do bear a brain. He was a merry man. I warrant I should live a thousand years, I never would forget him!"

"Nurse, be quiet!" said Eager.

The nurse pursed her lips and looked down at her lap. The interrogator replaced her stylus in the lexiscreen. "Well, that concludes—"

"Yet I cannot choose but laugh to think of him!" said the nurse, chuckling.

Eager glared at her, and she fell silent again.

"That concludes our session, for today," said the woman.

"Will there be others?" said Eager.

The woman raised her eyebrows. "If we decide that you are really extraterrestrials, we shall have many more questions to ask!" She rose. "I will go and write up this report for the general. I shall leave you here for tonight. Is there anything you need?"

"No, thank you," said Eager. "We will turn down our power and rest."

The woman nodded and left the room. As soon as the door closed behind her, Jonquil jumped from Eager's back and performed a succession of starbursts. "Well done, Uncle Eager!"

"And well done, Nurse," said Eager. "It was a good thing you remembered your friend Leo—" He stopped, in case he set off another train of reminiscences.

"Uncle Eager," said Jonquil, his radiating points spinning cartwheels on the table. "Now that you've been debriefed, shall I go and find out about Sam?"

"Yes," said Eager, pleased. Everything seemed to be going to plan.

CHAPTER 43

Spherelike, Jonquil rolled and hopped along corridors, following Molly's directions. The floor was spotlessly clean, so he was able to gather speed. The corridors were dark, and he was too insubstantial to trigger the light sensors. His sight depended on radar and sonar in any case, and he negotiated the twists and turns with ease.

Eventually he came to a corridor with a series of doors. He counted to the third one, flattened himself and slipped beneath it. He emerged in a room with only a gobetween and several chairs.

Though the gobetween appeared like any other he had seen, Jonquil already sensed that it had immense power. Hundreds of his cilia detached themselves and entered the control box. A minute later, they reappeared and attached themselves to Jonquil. He hopped to the door, compressed himself and went to find Eager.

* * * * *

The interrogator hurried down a corridor toward a discreet door at the far end. She waited for the door to recognize her and let her in. A man in pajamas and dressing gown sat behind a desk in the center of the room. He was gaunt-faced, though powerfully built. He looked up and frowned.

"I'm sorry, General," the woman said breathlessly. "The debriefing took rather longer than I expected."

"What are your conclusions?" said the general without to-do.

"Definitely intelligent life."

The general nodded. "That will be all."

The woman shifted her feet. "Sir, if I may say something more . . . They claim to have been invited here by Leonardo da Vinci."

"Leonardo da Vinci!"

"Yes, General. I've just checked on the gobetween, and it says he was interested in astronomy. We know that there were treatises on extraterrestrials during the Renaissance. If people were writing about such things, might they not have asked Leonardo to send a signal into space, in the same way they commissioned him to paint a picture or build a war machine? He was so far ahead of his time."

"Very plausible," said the general. "He was certainly a man of ideas. But did he ever build a helicopter, or a diving bell? How could he have used radio waves four centuries before Hertz first detected them and Marconi first transmitted them?"

"You're right, General." The woman hurried forward and

placed her lexiscreen on the desk. She turned to go. Then she paused.

"There is one other thing," she said.

"Yes?"

"I asked my questions as objectively as I could. Some of my observations may surprise you. . . ."

"Surprise me now," said the general. He yawned.

The woman was used to the general's forthrightness. "In my view, these robots are more than intelligent. They display emotional behavior, empathy and self-reflection. And possibly—though I wasn't too sure of this—humor."

The general did not speak for some seconds. His face was impassive. "Thank you, that will be all."

The woman had reached the door when he said, "Is Major Campbell back yet?"

"Not until tomorrow," said the woman. "Good night, General."

The general leant over the desk and picked up the lexiscreen. "I'll read this before I go to bed. I take it no one else knows?"

"Apart from the security guards who brought them to me, no," said the woman. She left the room and walked back along the corridor. Sensing her presence, lights came on. The click-clacking of her heels against the floor broke the silence of the night. It was so late that only the personnel at the gates remained on duty. As she passed the corridor to the top-security room, she heard a noise like someone stepping on autumn leaves. She stopped and looked over her shoulder, but the corridor was in darkness. She shook her head and went on her way.

⸬ ⸬ ⸬ ⸬ ⸬

"Uncle Eager!" A wafer-thin projectile shot from under the door and landed at Eager's feet. The nurse, who was slumped against the wall on minimum power, gave a start. She sat back and resumed her impression of sleep. "Uncle Eager, I've found out all about Sam." Jonquil became a straw-colored ball. "Molly was right. There was an unexplained signal last weekend when Sam was at the listening station, and he is being debriefed. But he isn't on the moon, he's at the International Space Station."

"So he's still in space?" said Eager.

"Yes. They won't send him home until the signal has been investigated."

"Is he all right?"

"Yes. But the report said he was tired after his traveling and the debriefing."

"I can understand that," said Eager. "Thank you, Jonquil. Now we must wait for Molly to arrive in the morning. Then we can go home." He sat down beside the nurse. "I'm going to turn down my power and process my thoughts," he said. "You probably need to regain energy too."

The ball settled on the floor and rested in silence.

CHAPTER 44

Early the next day, the sun was warm enough for Ju and Finbar to swim in the outdoor pool. Afterward, they had breakfast with Gavin before leaving to visit the space center.

As the hovercar stopped in the parking lot, Ju finally said what was on her mind. "Uncle Gavin, have you spoken to Molly?"

"I called her while you were swimming," said Gavin. "She's been listening to the local news, and there's no report of strange robots being found, which suggests that they're at ISA. Molly's on her way there now."

"So we should soon know about Dad," said Ju, her heart quickening.

They stepped out of the car and looked around. Though the countryside was hilly and verdant, the gray rocks created austere shadows. Bright splashes of color came not from the landscape but from the vehicles parked at the space center.

The building was a large white dome, reached by a stone

path. Finbar stopped halfway and gazed into the hills. "Is this where you came to drop Eager and the nurse?"

"That's right. ISA is further down the road. But let's try and forget about what's happening while we're here. I've always wanted to come to the space center," said Gavin. He smiled, but he could not hide the anxiety in his eyes.

As they followed her uncle through the main door, Ju whispered to Finbar, "He's worried about Molly." Finbar nodded in agreement. Inside the building, crowds of people were finding their way among the many signs and exhibits.

"Shall we hire a guide?" said Gavin, pointing to several animats in space suits.

"Who needs a guide when you have me?" cried Ju. "If there's one thing I've learnt about, it's space."

Gavin grinned—genuinely this time. "Let's find a gobeyhall and you can take us."

＊ ＊ ＊ ＊ ＊

Eager had just turned up his power when the nurse stirred. "What a slugabed I am, Sir Fie!" she exclaimed. She stood up and went to the door. "I must go and wake my lady Juliet."

The door ignored her approach. "Nay, open!" she cried.

"I think it must be locked," said Eager. "But Lady Juliet is not here, anyway. You must sit down and wait."

"Locked?" said Jonquil's voice. Paper-shaped, he hopped in

front of Eager. "Then you won't be able to help me with my plan."

"Your plan?" said Eager. "But we've already carried out our plan, and when Molly comes, we can tell her about Sam and go home."

The paper swayed as if it could not hold itself still. "I've had a better idea! Since we know where Sam is, why don't we get him sent home now?"

Eager stared at his nephew. "How?"

"The gobetween I entered last night is a separate machine from the other gobetweens. It holds important and secret information that they don't know about. And it has a special section for giving orders."

"Can you give it an order to release Sam?" said Eager.

"I think so," said Jonquil with uncharacteristic hesitancy. "I didn't stay inside for long, but I felt that this part of the machine is hard to enter."

"Molly didn't suggest this," said Eager, "so I don't think we should try."

Jonquil gave a flutter. "Molly only thinks you can pick up signals from machines. She doesn't know about me and what I can do."

Eager tilted his head. His nephew was right. Molly had not suggested that he do any more, because she had thought it impossible.

"Why do you need my help?" he said.

"I want you to come into the room with me, because I may

need to send more cilia into the machine. Afterward, I may be too weak to leave by myself," said Jonquil.

"This is too much for you to do," said Eager.

"No! I want to help the girl and her mother. Don't you?"

Eager thought of Ju and Fleur and their anxious faces as they said goodbye to him. "Yes. But if this door is locked, I can't go with you. Let's wait until Molly comes. I can tell her the plan and pretend that I can do it—" Jonquil became an arrow and shot across the room, landing on the bench beside the nurse. She drew back in alarm.

"There's no time, Uncle Eager! Outside are lots of corridors and doors, so there must be lots of people who work here. I must go before they arrive."

Before Eager could protest, the arrow fired itself into the space under the door. "Jonquil . . . ," said Eager hopelessly.

There was a knock on the door, and Molly entered.

"Eager!" she cried. "You were magnificent."

Eager was staring at the door. "It was locked," he said.

"I know the master code," said Molly offhandedly.

"I've found out about Sam," said Eager before she could continue.

Molly looked startled. "Already? I was going to take you to the room—"

Eager said hastily, "I tuned in to the information from here, perhaps because it was so quiet in the night. You were right about everything. And I found out that Sam is being debriefed at the International Space Station."

"Of course, I should have known they'd take him there," said Molly. "I'll pass on the news to Gavin tonight. Fleur will be so relieved."

"Won't we see Gavin ourselves tonight?" said Eager. An uneasiness came over him.

Molly seemed not to have heard the question. "I've read the report, Eager, and you did better than I ever expected!" she said. "Dr. Shu almost believes that you're extraterrestrials. The general will be delighted!" She paused. Her cheeks were flushed and her eyes ablaze. Eager tilted his head again. There was something unexpected in what Molly had just said. . . .

She went on, "What makes it hard to disprove your story is that robots like you aren't supposed to exist on Earth. Scientists are banned from building self-aware robots. So you must have come from outer space!"

It struck Eager that Molly had never described him as self-aware before. "Did Gavin tell you about me?" he said.

Molly smiled as if she was amused. "I knew about you long before I met Gavin. I didn't know that he had any connection with you. But the moment I saw you at his parents' house, I recognized you."

She moved nearer to him, looking into his eyes. "Did you know who *I* was, Eager?" she said softly.

Eager was about to shake his head, but Molly said, "I wondered, you see, how good your pattern recognition would be."

It was true that her face had revived a memory in Eager. He had felt it stir the first time they met; and when she was talking to him on the train, his mind had been reaching for something just beyond its grasp. Now, as she faced him, he let his thoughts float back through the years, his memory searching for the missing link. . . .

"Mr. Lobsang," he murmured, startling himself with his own utterance.

"My grandfather," said Molly just as quietly. For a split second, to Eager's eyes, the slant of Molly's cheekbones and the outline of her jaw became the face of a Tibetan man. The image passed.

Molly said, "You saved my grandfather's life twenty years ago. The robots he had built would have killed him, and you rescued him. I was a child at the time, but he made me and my parents promise to do all we could to help you, if it was ever necessary." She smiled. "All along, you have had more friends than the Bells and Professor Ogden."

At the mention of the professor's name, Eager's system did an internal somersault. But it was natural that Molly would know of him. Though younger, Professor Ogden had been a colleague of her grandfather.

"I'm very grateful to your family," Eager said.

"When I was a student, I campaigned against the Ban," said Molly. "It was my way of helping you. I never imagined that I would actually meet you one day." She smiled again. "You're just as my grandfather described you. Not only your appearance, but your understanding and human sensibilities. As for being a threat to us"—she gave a hollow laugh—"it's other people we should worry about, not robots like you."

Eager stepped back. "Shall we go now?" He was thinking that he could summon Jonquil.

But Molly had not finished speaking. "That's why I brought you here," she said.

Eager's system jumped again. "To find out about Sam?" he said.

"That was my first idea," said Molly. "I only wanted to help Fleur. But when I left her house the other night to consider my plan, I realized that there were far more important things we could do!"

Eager took another step back. "I don't understand," he said.

"I'm more senior than I told Gavin," said Molly, to Eager's bewilderment. "I'm the general's close aide. I understand how his mind works. He sees his mission as more than going into space. He believes that space offers possibilities to shape the human race. But he hasn't been able to do anything about it, until now."

The jinn on her belt buzzed. "The general is on his way," it announced.

"He'll explain it to you," Molly said. She frowned thoughtfully. "You know, I imagine he's not unlike Professor Ogden. He's a man of vision. He believes in the fundamental goodness of human nature."

She looked as if she might say more, but the door opened and the general entered.

CHAPTER 45

The corridors were busy with people. More than once Jonquil blended with the ceiling to avoid being seen. The final corridor of doors was much quieter. Once again, he rolled and hopped along the pristine floor. Two men were in the third room. Jonquil sensed them, leaning over the gobetween, the moment he slipped under the door. He lay there, flat as a sheet of paper, while he considered where to hide. The door opened and a pair of sharp-pointed feet strode over him, just missing him. Still paperlike, Jonquil scuttled on fibrous legs toward the back of the gobetween.

"Has any more information been received about the signals?" said a woman's voice. It was Dr. Shu, the interrogator. Jonquil felt her energy struggling between excitement and wariness.

"No," said one of the men. "We're still waiting for an analysis of the likely source." He stepped away from the machine to continue his conversation with the woman. The other man remained by the gobetween, examining data on the screen. He failed to spot an insect entering the control box.

Jonquil's cilia quickly returned to the circuitry where they had read the information about Sam. From there, they moved deeper into the machine, sensing that few people ever had access to this part.

At the very center, they hit a solid wall. Closer examination showed that it was a crystalline structure, a lattice of interconnecting molecules. The cilia split into smaller parts and were able to slip through the gaps in the lattice.

They spread out, feeling information pulsing around them, noting its ebbs and surges; at times, merging with a passing wave and unlocking its secret. The cilia told Jonquil that each bit of information held part of a message. But the pieces were muddled up and moving so fast that it was impossible to read them as a whole.

Jonquil understood that the lattice received information from outside and encrypted it. The message he wanted to send about Sam was short enough to slip through the system, but without official authorization it would be rejected. He told the cilia, "You must find the end of a message with the general's name so I can attach my order to it."

He waited some time for a response. Dr. Shu finished her conversation with the man. Jonquil heard her heels clicking as she left the room. The man at the gobetween stood up and stretched his arms. "I need a break," he said.

"Not yet," said his colleague. "We have to get everything sent today."

Jonquil's cilia-antennae had found a fragment containing the general's name and a hologram of a walrus. "That's what I need," said Jonquil. "Now, this is my message, to go above the general's seal: 'Release Sam Hudson. Return him to Earth ee–' " Jonquil paused.

He had never seen the word to learn the spelling, and it was a long one. "Eemmeadiatly," he told the cilia. He reviewed this and changed it to "immeediatly." He tried "immeadiatly" and "eemeediatly" and was still not satisfied. "At once," he said. Inside the lattice, the cilia began to vibrate in synchrony, inserting the pattern of Jonquil's message into the general's memo.

"Done," said the man who had been talking with Dr. Shu. "Now we can take a break." Both men turned away from the gobetween and left the room.

"Hooray!" Jonquil thought. "Success!"

CHAPTER 46

"**I'm not one to beat** about the bush," said the general. He stood in the middle of the room, tall and imposing in his uniform. The nurse bobbed a curtsy.

"I've read the report on you," the general continued, "and it's clear to me that you're remarkable robots, wherever you come from. I have a proposition for you. It will cover you with glory and help save the world. What do you think?"

Eager said, "Would you mind explaining the proposition?"

The general sat down on a chair, keeping his military bearing. "We like to think we're progressing, here on Earth, what with all our technology and psychology, and understanding of the universe. But what good is it doing us if we still devastate the planet and divide ourselves into the haves and the have-nots?"

He paused, but Eager had an inkling that he did not require an answer. The man continued, "Even though we have clean fuel today, we're still polluting and using up the planet's resources as if there's no tomorrow. Perhaps one day there *will* be no tomorrow!"

He glanced at Molly. "That's where space comes into it. Governments hope that we'll be able to find other habitable environments in space. We can all move into the universe, lock, stock and barrel."

He said this in such a way that Eager was unsure whether he agreed with the idea or not.

"Now, I'm not saying folks are evil," said the general. Eager tilted his head, increasing his thinking power to follow this new train of thought.

"I think people are essentially kind. But love and kindness aren't enough. Sometimes you have to take action, to change the big things. Do you know, our basic ways of doing things have not changed for centuries? Some people still make money just sitting on their backsides. Others scrape and toil and still starve. I'm a plain-speaking man, Eager, as you can tell."

"That doesn't sound very fair," said Eager, who felt that a comment was called for.

"Fairness! Now you've put your finger on it. Our way of doing things is not fair. Every child knows that. They grow up learning about the state of the world, and they say, 'That isn't fair.' And they're right. But over time they get the message, 'That's the way it is, and that's the way it's going to stay.' "

He looked over at Molly again. "Religion can't help. It has done its best, but it can't change our institutions today. What we need is leadership. Imagine if God said, 'Now change this.' Wouldn't we all run to obey? We couldn't make excuses anymore. Now, God, if there's such a thing, isn't speaking to us in a way that we can all hear. But if another voice, a wiser voice, spoke to us from beyond . . ." He broke off and looked intently in Eager's direction.

The robot glanced around the room, but the general's gaze was definitely on him. "Me?" he said.

The general nodded. "That's right, Sir Fic. I want you to lead us back to the Garden of Eden."

Eager was taken aback. Take everyone into a garden? "Will there be room?" he said.

"It's a metaphorical garden," said the general with a frown. "It goes back to the time when men and women lived in harmony with each other. We didn't have any institutions then, like governments and world banks and armies."

"You mean you would like to start again?" said Eager.

"That's it," said the general. "With a little help from Maoz."

Eager looked at the nurse, who was watching the general reverently from the bench. "Do you think people will believe that we're from Maoz?" he said.

The general stood up. "If the International Space Authority says it's an extraterrestrial, it's an extraterrestrial," he said. "I may have my own doubts, but I'm not one to look a gift horse in the mouth. And Molly here tells me that no one on Earth is likely to stand up and claim that they built you." He walked to the door. "I'll leave you to think about this awhile; then I'll be back to discuss what we can do."

The nurse jumped from the bench and curtsied to the man's retreating figure. "O Lord, I could have stayed here all the day to hear good counsel. O, what learning is!"

Eager turned to Molly. "Why did you say that, Molly?"

She looked surprised. "Say what?"

"That no one on Earth would claim to have built me. You meant Professor Ogden."

"Yes," said Molly. "You must know that he can't confess. He would go to prison, and his life's work would be at an end. You would be destroyed, if we couldn't save you somehow. But that isn't the real reason I said that." Molly's eyes were bright with passion. She went on, "I don't believe Professor Ogden would want to spoil the general's plan, because I'm sure he would agree with it. The general is not a bad man; he doesn't want to be a world leader, he just wants to put a stop to injustice. Doesn't Professor Ogden want to do the same thing? Wouldn't he be proud of you, if you helped to bring it about?"

"Professor Ogden is a good man too," Eager said. "I know he wants to change things. Shall I ask him what he thinks?"

Molly raised an eyebrow. "Eager, do you think the general will wait while you contact Professor Ogden? Why do you need to ask him? You've just told me the answer."

"I suppose I have," said Eager. He gave a chuckle, and Molly laughed with him.

After Molly had left the room, Eager said to the nurse, "Jonquil needn't have gone to send a message. I could probably ask the general to release Sam, now that we're working together."

The nurse clapped her hand to her mouth in admiration.

CHAPTER 47

Something was wrong in the gobetween. The moment the door closed behind the technicians, Jonquil summoned his cilia to return. It had taken them a while to send the message to release Sam, and he was impatient to sense himself whole again.

The cilia-antennae did not emerge. For several seconds Jonquil knew only that they were scattering in all directions. His energy surged as the cilia divided, swiveled, reeled and raced around the gaps in the lattice.

At last, brief signals came: "Exits blocked . . . attackers . . ."

Jonquil sent more cilia into the gobetween. They reached the first level of circuitry. From there, they detected waves of molecular activity from an unknown source. Immubots had descended on the lattice to destroy the intruders.

Once more the cilia in the lattice pressed to the exits; some of them made their way through. Hordes of immubots enclosed them, as if in a bubble.

"Rescue them!" said Jonquil to the new detachment of cilia.

Already they had formed themselves into wings. The cilia-insects dived toward the attackers, like hornets into an ants' nest. The bubble around the cilia-antennae burst, flinging immubots against the walls of the circuitry's casing. The cilia flew to freedom. The cilia left behind in the lattice darted through the gaps, where the winged cilia waited to defend them.

Jonquil felt energy drain from him and knew that he must hold on to what little remained. One by one, the cilia returned to him. His power had gone. Pale and crushed, he lay on the floor behind the gobetween.

The two men returned from their break and began checking that the messages had been sent and received. There was a bleeping at the door.

"Cleaner," said one of the men. "It isn't allowed in here unsupervised."

"We might as well let it in," said his colleague. The cleaner, which had been sucking up dust and particles from the corridors, maneuvered itself into the room. Starting at the far end, behind the gobetween machine, it gathered everything in its wake into its belly. It detected an object, whitish and crumpled on the floor. The sensor relayed the information for processing. "Crumpled" signified unusable; "floor" that the object had been discarded.

The machine swept toward Jonquil.

CHAPTER 48

For several hours Eager and the nurse were left alone in the interrogation room. Eager knew that some robots did not mind long stretches with nothing to do, but he soon felt bored. The nurse busied herself rehearsing a song about a cuckoo and another about herbs.

Eager concentrated on sending a message to Jonquil, but his nephew did not reply. To take his mind off his growing anxiety, Eager thought about the few days they had just spent together. How insistent Jonquil had been that he was ready to go out into the world! But it turned out that all his knowledge of life was based on the fictitious Jones family. Then Eager's memory took him back to the Bells' living room, when he had overheard Fleur's happy excitement as she invited Gavin to the house. Later, when she learnt the truth about the simulated Sam, she'd been angry and sad about the deception.

For a large part of the day, these thoughts went round and round in Eager's head, as if searching for a resting place. At last he came to a resolution and stilled his mind.

"Nurse," he said, "would you like to teach me a song? We could sing it together."

Eager had learnt to sing when he lived with the Bells. He enjoyed it, though he could never match the gusto of humans, who seemed to find a particular pleasure in unleashing their voices.

"Will you sing 'Hey nonny no'?" said the nurse.

"Whatever you wish," said Eager.

When Molly entered, she found them skipping down the room, hand in hand, singing at the top of their voices:

"Hey nonny no!

Men are fools that wish to die!

Is't not fine to dance and sing,

When the bells of death do ring?

Is't not fine to swim in wine,

And turn upon the toe,

And sing hey nonny no!

When the winds blow, and the seas flow?

Hey nonny no!"

They turned on their toes and sang again, for good measure, "Hey nonny no."

Eager caught sight of Molly and dropped the nurse's hand.

"I am aweary," said the nurse. "Give me leave a while." She ambled over to the bench.

"The general wants to see you!" Molly said. "I'm to take you to his office."

"Molly, I've changed my mind," said Eager.

Her mouth fell open. "Why?"

"It would be wrong to pretend to be something I'm not."

"You're pretending now," retorted Molly.

"Not for long," said Eager, "and only because you said it didn't matter. But the general wants to present me to the world as an extraterrestrial, and it will matter whether people believe me or not."

"Of course it will matter!" cried Molly. "For a good end!"

Eager shook his head. "It won't be true, and therefore it could never be right."

"Right?" said Molly scornfully. "Don't you think the general wants to do what's right? You must understand his aim. We're not an advanced civilization. We're fooling ourselves if we think we are, while we still fight and destroy the planet. We need a messenger from a higher civilization to explain to us what we're doing wrong."

"They won't believe me," said Eager. "Humans will want to test me, to ask me questions, debrief me. . . ."

Molly smiled. "We'll brief you better this time. Your story will be flawless. Eager, do you understand the significance of the International Space Authority?"

"No," said Eager.

"Space travel began as a race between countries to prove they had superior technology. But it's absurd to think that a single country can lay claim to the universe. So nations have learnt to cooperate in space. Now they need to cooperate on Earth, to look after the planet as a whole and share its resources. To do that, everyone needs the same vision. We must all follow the same guide."

She looked pleadingly at him. "Do you understand?"

Eager nodded. "But I cannot be the guide," he said. "If people are going to cooperate, surely they must tell each other the truth? How can the general ask them to do that if he's telling them a lie about me?"

He tilted his head and tried to think of an image: he knew that humans liked thinking in pictures. "You wouldn't build a house with a wobbly base," he said.

"Sometimes the end does justify the means," said Molly. She sounded sad. "Didn't Professor Ogden make you in our image so that you could help humans?"

"I've been thinking," said Eager. "Professor Ogden believes that people should be told the truth. He only keeps me hidden for my own safety. He would not agree with the general." The robot added, "Neither would Gavin."

"Gavin?" said Molly in surprise.

"Once, Gavin explained to me the difference between small lies and deception," said Eager.

"I'm sure Gavin would understand the general's vision," said Molly. She did not sound very sure at all.

"I'm sorry," said Eager, seeing how disappointed Molly looked.

She ran her fingers through her hair. "The general will be angry . . . ," she said.

"I'll go and apologize to him," said Eager.

"Angry with *me*," said Molly. "But don't worry, I'll explain to him."

A thought struck Eager. "Will he let us go?"

Molly turned at the door, an expression of alarm flitting over her face. She smiled brightly. "Of course he will."

CHAPTER 49

Finbar sat facing Gavin and Ju in the cafeteria of the space center. They had just eaten reconstituted space food—an apple cake that tasted surprisingly good.

Gavin said, "Well, I take my hat off to the early space explorers. They set off with a fraction of the technology we have. Molly says our ID shields have more computer power than the machine that ran the moon missions."

Ju sneaked a smile at Finbar. They had noticed that her uncle took every opportunity to mention Molly. But Finbar seemed lost in thought. He said, "We haven't overcome the rules of physics, though, have we? I mean, we can't beam people through space, travel faster than the speed of light or alter gravity."

"My dad can fly!" said Ju. "Well, on the moon he can. He puts on wings in the exercise hall. Because the room's full of oxygen and he's a sixth of his body weight, he can flap his wings and off he goes."

"I experienced weightlessness on the Sorbjet," said Finbar. "That was strange. Especially having conversations with people, just floating there. I talked to a man who had been to the moon. He was a scientist, he looked the eccentric type, with thick white hair—"

Gavin cried out, "What was his name?"

"I don't know," said Finbar.

Was the man famous after all? He and the scientist had not bothered to introduce themselves; they were just chatting as strangers. But Finbar had introduced himself to the boy, and the boy had deliberately withheld his name. . . .

". . . sounds like him," Gavin was saying.

Finbar realized that he had missed some of the conversation. "Sounds like who?" he said.

"You said the scientist you met went to the moon?" said Gavin.

"Yes, for his work."

"It must be Professor Ogden," said Gavin.

Finbar frowned. Hadn't he heard the name before?

Sounding excited, Gavin said, "He was on your flight? He arrived when you did?"

"I don't think he bailed out before we landed," said Finbar dryly.

Gavin laughed. "I'm just finding this hard to believe. Mum and Dad thought he was away traveling. I'll tell them he's back. He might be able to shed some light on what's happening."

Ju and Finbar were looking inquiringly at him. "Professor Ogden has contacts in high places," said Gavin. He sipped his coffee. He was clearly not going to say any more.

Finbar asked Ju as they left the building, "Who is this professor?"

Ju stared at him. "Don't you know? Mum says he built Eager." Of course! Marcia had told Finbar the same thing.

When they left, it was growing dark. As they climbed into the hovercar, Gavin's jinn buzzed. "You have a call from Molly."

"Molly! Is everything OK?"

Molly's voice sounded strained. "Yes, yes. My first day back went like a dream." This was their code for Molly to tell him that Sam was safe.

Gavin put his free arm around his niece and hugged her.

"Shall we meet, then?" he said. If Molly said yes, it meant that she would have the robots with her.

"Yes," said Molly in a subdued tone.

"This evening? At the hotel?" said Gavin.

"No, now," said Molly. "Can you come here? Stop at the turning to the main road and wait for me there."

"All right," said Gavin. He wanted to say more, but they had agreed that it would be unwise. "See you in half an hour."

"Is something wrong?" said Finbar from the backseat.

"I think she must be tired," said Gavin. "After all, Molly's carried all this in her head. Goodness knows what she had to do today."

"Your dad is safe, Ju!" said Finbar.

"Yes," said Ju without turning round. She was wiping away a tear.

CHAPTER 58

The door of the interrogation room opened and Molly came in. Eager was hitting a ball against the wall with a wooden spoon. The ball bounced off, feebly, and dropped in front of Molly. She saw that it was a rolled-up sock.

"The nurse is teaching me how to play," Eager said. He retrieved the sock.

"Eager, there's no time to lose," said Molly. "I've told the general what you said and he's furious. This evening he's going to think about what to do with you."

"Do with me?"

Molly hurried to the door. "I'm taking you away from here. I've promised to keep you safe, remember? Gavin is going to meet us."

Gavin! Eager's system felt a surge of pleasure. "Come, Nurse," he said. He dropped the sock and spoon back in her apron pocket. At the door he stopped, his happiness turning to alarm. Where was Jonquil?

Gavin took the hovercar in the opposite direction to the town and stopped at the junction to the main road. "This is where Molly told us to wait. Shall we have some music?"

Ju yawned. "I shouldn't be sleepy," she said. "I've got to stay awake and hear what Molly says about Dad."

Gavin's jinn buzzed. "Molly!" he cried, pulling back his sleeve before the jinn could announce her.

"Gavin! I don't know what to do!"

Gavin kept his voice steady. "Is there a problem?"

"It's Eager. He won't come."

"Won't come?"

Ju swiveled round in her seat to exchange glances with Finbar.

Molly said, "He refuses. I tried to pull him out of the room, but he wrapped one of his legs around the table."

"Why?" said Gavin.

"I don't understand him," said Molly. "You must talk to him. . . . Here he is."

"Eager, what's the matter?" said Gavin.

The robot's face appeared on the jinn screen. He said, "I'm not ready to go."

"But Molly said you've found out about Sam. . . ."

"I'm waiting for something else," said the robot.

"What?" said Gavin.

261

"I'm very sorry, Gavin. I've told Molly she should leave me. If the general decides what to do with me, I shall have to decide what to do with myself."

"I don't understand," said Gavin. He rubbed his forehead as he spoke. "It's been a long day for us all. Perhaps you're not thinking very clearly. Come with Molly now."

"I can't." In the interrogation room, Eager sat on the floor, holding Molly's jinn in his hand. The nurse was sitting on a bench, wringing her hands. Molly stood, looking down at Eager with quizzical eyes. He handed the jinn back to her.

Molly spoke into it. "Gavin, I'll try to bring Eager. If not, I'll meet you shortly with the nurse. I'm sorry, I've done my best!"

She turned back to Eager. "If you insist on staying, I shall leave you. But if the general comes to find you . . ."

"I shall have to speak to him," said Eager. "But I can't go now."

"Come, Nurse," said Molly. She went to the door and it opened.

The animat limped over to Eager. "O courteous Sir Fie, honest gentleman," she cried. "That ever I should live to see thee dead!"

"Nurse, you must go with Molly," said Eager.

A squelching noise and the swish of a brush was heard outside the door. Molly gave a start and stepped into the corridor. "Only the cleaner," she said with relief. "Eager, this is your last chance. . . ."

The sounds came closer, interspersed with a faint cry of "Uncle . . ."

Eager bounded to the door, stretching the leg that was entwined around the table.

"Jonquil?" he thought as he peered round the door.

"Uncle Ea . . ."

Eager looked up and down the corridor, taking in the ceiling and the floor. "Jonquil, where are you?" he thought.

"There's nothing to harm you," said Molly. Her voice softened. "Is that what you were afraid of, that it would be unsafe to leave the room?"

Eager did not respond. He was straining to hear from Jonquil. The cleaner swished past the door. "Uncle Eag . . ." The feeble cry sounded nearer.

"Jonquil?" thought Eager.

"For the last time, Eager, it's perfectly safe. Will you come along?" cried Molly.

"Here . . . ," said a wisp of a voice.

Eager looked at the departing cleaner with horror. Had Jonquil been sucked inside it? He released his leg from the table and went into the corridor.

"Thank goodness," said Molly. "Come on. Quickly!" She walked briskly ahead of Eager, past the slowly progressing cleaner.

Eager pointed to the machine. "Nurse, open it," he whispered.

"Nay, Sir Fie—"

"Do as I say!" hissed Eager.

The nurse bent down and lunged at the cleaner with out-stretched hands. It slipped from her grasp, emitting a shrill bleep.

Molly turned round. "What on earth . . . ?"

"Come back!" cried the nurse. Pouncing again, she clasped her hands firmly round the cleaner and hugged it to her bosom.

"My husband, God be with his soul, he was a merry man. He could catch a pig—"

"That's a machine!" yelled Molly. She cringed as she realized that she had shouted. "Put it down," she said between clenched teeth. When the nurse did not obey, Molly turned to Eager. "Tell her to put it down," she said.

Eager hesitated, and Molly took hold of the cleaner. "Put it down." She wrestled it from the nurse's grip.

"Sir Fie!" cried the nurse.

The next moment she and Molly had disappeared under a gray cloud. A loud coughing was heard. Eager dived to the floor to examine the contents of the cleaner's stomach. There was dust, lots of it, and screwed up pieces of paper, discarded microchips, food wrappers, a button, unidentifiable metal bits . . .

"Jonquil!" thought Eager in despair.

Some of the dust particles started to gather together. Long gray strands, like odd bits of string, joined them.

The coughing subsided. "Oh, oh," said Molly's voice. She sounded very sorry for herself. Eager looked up and saw her rubbing her eyes. He turned back to the object emerging from the dust, willing it to hurry.

"What on earth's the matter with you two?" said Molly furiously. "I thought Eager was intelligent, at least. Now, put that machine down and follow me!"

Eager was impressed to see the nurse still clutching the cleaner. "Put it down, Nurse," he said. "And give your apron a shake."

A second cloud of dust rose in the air. Molly staggered backward, spluttering and covering her face with her hands. Unseen, Jonquil slipped into the pocket of the nurse's apron.

"   "   ⋕   ⋕   ⋕

Ten minutes later, a small flying pod and a truck arrived at the spot where Gavin and the children were waiting. As the pod came closer, they could see Molly at the controls and Eager and the nurse squashed beside her. The pod landed, and the truck pulled up in the middle of the road.

"Molly's got an escort," said Finbar. "How did she manage that?"

The passengers climbed out. Molly's face and clothes were streaked with dirt. The nurse was no better. Her headdress and apron were the color of smoke.

"What's happened?" exclaimed Ju.

Gavin climbed out of the car. "Molly!" he cried. He went to hug her. But she shook her head and indicated the waiting truck. Two men sat impassively in the front seat. "Who are they?" he said.

"Patrolmen. Friends of Eager and the nurse, apparently," whispered Molly. "They insisted on accompanying us."

"Are you all right?" said Gavin. "You look . . ."

"I'm fine," she croaked.

"Will you join us tonight to celebrate?"

Molly swallowed. "I can't. And you mustn't stay any longer. Take the night train home. I'm sorry, Gavin."

"What for?" said Gavin, stepping closer to her. "What's happened?"

She drew back. "I can't explain. Eager will tell you. He said you wouldn't agree with me, and he was right. There are things you and I could never agree on. I see that now."

"Tell me what's happened!" cried Gavin.

Molly's eyes were moist. "I've been demoted," she said. "The general is sending me to another division."

"I'm so sorry," said Gavin. "But what about . . . ?"

"I must go." Molly turned away. She came back and kissed Gavin on the cheek. "I'm sorry."

Eager and the nurse had been waiting by the car to say good-bye to Molly, but she hardly glanced at them. They climbed into the backseat with Finbar.

Gavin got in beside Ju. She glanced at her uncle and saw a

stunned look on his face. He brushed dust from his cheek and stared at it for a moment.

The drone of the flying pod filled the air. It took off and headed back. The truck followed. As they drove off, the driver and his passenger waved, shouting through the open window, *"Salutations à Maoz!"*

CHAPTER 51

The hovercar glided along the road, toward the lights of the town. Darkness had come swiftly.

Eager waited until he thought Jonquil would be recovered, then asked in his mind, "Are you all right? What happened?"

The reply from the nurse's apron was just audible. "I lost power sending the message. There were immubots guarding the gobetween. They attacked me. . . . Then a machine swallowed me. . . ."

"A cleaner," thought Eager. "How did it do that?"

"I broke up as it sucked me in," said Jonquil. He must have sensed Eager's horror, for he said, "Don't worry, Uncle Eager. You know I can detach parts easily. I'm designed to come to pieces."

"But your fibers could have been crushed," said Eager.

"I'm too flexible."

"And you are sensitive to dust particles."

"Yes." Jonquil was silent for a moment. "I was a bit scared, Uncle Eager. But I think because they were separated, my fibers were undamaged. Had I been whole, the dust would have entered my connections." In a stronger voice he said, "I sent the message. I told the authorities to send Sam home . . ." He paused. "At once."

"Well done," said Eager.

"Uncle Gavin," said Ju, "will you stop for a moment?" They were driving across a vast plain, empty of anything but trees. "I want to show Eager something."

Everyone climbed out, except for the nurse, who sat slumped in the back of the car, and Jonquil.

Ju led Eager away from the glare of the car headlights. They passed shrubs and rocks. The soil beneath Eager's feet was dry and crumbly. Chirruping crickets drowned out the silence.

"Look," Ju said, pointing to the night sky. "Those bright lights beside the moon—that's the International Space Station, where my dad is. Thank you for helping us, Eager. I know what a risk you took. My mum explained all about you and the Ban." She smiled ruefully. "I'm sorry I ignored you in the past."

"You were meant to ignore me," said Eager. He gazed up at the moon, which was almost at its fullest. With his acute eyesight, he saw dark patches against the blond surface.

"See the stars?" said Ju. "That's where you come from."

"I'm not really from Maoz," said Eager.

Ju laughed. "I didn't mean that."

Eager had an urge to show Jonquil the huge panorama of the sky. "I'll fetch the nurse," he said, striding off to the car.

The nurse came, protesting. "Jesu, what haste. Do you not see that I am out of breath?"

"Jonquil," thought Eager, "look at the stars." Wan-colored fibers poked out of the nurse's apron.

Finbar and Gavin, who had been standing apart, joined the others.

"We're all of us extraterrestrials, aren't we?" said Ju to her uncle.

Gavin grinned. "I suppose we are, when you think that the particles in our body were once scattered across the universe."

"But I'm a robot," said Eager.

"It's true for you as well," said Gavin. "Every atom heavier than hydrogen—and you are made of plenty of those—came from inside a long-dead star that exploded, sending out matter that eventually formed planets."

"We're stardust, that's what my dad says," said Ju.

They stood side by side, looking at the constellations, until Gavin said, "We'd better go."

Finbar noticed that the nurse had moved some way off. "Nurse, come back!" he called.

As she stumbled across the ground, a flash of light fell toward her, appearing to strike her.

"What was that?" cried Ju.

"A shooting star, I expect," said Finbar.

¤ ¤ ¤ ¤ ¤

The hovercar stopped outside a hotel with lemon trees framing the entrance. The street was full of people enjoying a stroll.

"We'll just fetch our bags, then we'll go to the railway station," said Gavin to the robots.

"Come with me, Nurse," said Ju. Her uncle looked inquiringly at her. "She can pack for me. There's something I have to do instead. I'll be very quick."

"We only have five minutes," said Gavin as they walked into the hotel.

"Thanks! I'll be in the gobeyhall," called Ju, running in the opposite direction.

The gobeyhall was free. She called up her story about the huntress. Bent double, the girl was moving stealthily through long grass. Her spear was at an angle, so that it sliced through the rushes. Ahead of her was the koala. He stopped, sniffed and changed course. The rushes closed behind him. The girl followed in his tracks.

"He's helping her hunt," Ju told herself. Aloud she said, "Gobey, the girl has found her kill for today. It's the koala."

There was a rustling from the screen. For an instant, Ju thought that the koala was going to thrust his way through the grass and confront her. "I don't need to see it happen, Gobey. But let that finish the story," she said quickly.

She heard footsteps behind her. "We're ready," said Finbar's voice. "I supervised your packing. . . ." He stepped closer, exclaiming, "Are you working on your story?"

"Finishing it," said Ju. "That koala took it over, just like ISA

271

took over my dad. I want it to stop." She turned to face Finbar. "I don't know what to believe anymore. Everything on the go-between could be made up or just there to sell me something."

"But it isn't," said Finbar. "You have to trust some things."

"I wish there was a way of telling," said Ju.

There was movement on the screen. The girl had quickened her pace. Her jaw was set and her spear raised. Ju looked away. "I have to kill him to remind myself he isn't real. He would be dead by now in real life, wouldn't he?"

Finbar shrugged. "Possibly. I don't know how tasty koala meat is. She'd kill him if she was desperate. Nice technology, that spear." His eyes were riveted to the screen.

"Come on," Ju urged. "We've a train to catch!"

The children and Gavin returned to the hovercar. "Are we going home now?" said Jonquil's voice from the nurse's apron.

"Yes," said Eager.

The car rose into the air. Gavin said, sounding more cheerful, "I've just called Fleur at home and told her that Sam is safe. You can imagine how happy she is. When we arrive tomorrow morning, we'll go straight to her house for breakfast. She wants to give you a hero's return, Eager."

CHAPTER 52

Early the next morning, an unusually lively party for the time of day took place above the dance school. Fleur ran across the terrace to greet the arrivals as they stepped from the lift.

"Mum!" cried Ju. "Dad's safe."

"I know." Fleur squeezed her daughter tight. She hugged Gavin, Finbar, Eager and even the nurse. "Thank you—all of you!" she cried. "Now come and sit down on the terrace and tell us all about it. Marcia's in the kitchen, making breakfast."

The nurse went into the house and reappeared with a tray of food. Marcia followed with a second tray. She kissed Finbar. "Hope you aren't too tired," she said. "We're going to your grandparents' later. I've packed your bags—they're in the car."

"Tell us everything that happened," Fleur was saying to Eager. "How did you find out about Sam? What did they say to you at ISA?"

"Hold on," said Gavin, helping himself to cereal. "We're not all here yet. Mum and Dad are on their way with a friend."

He grinned at Eager. "You'll never guess who. Professor Ogden is back."

"Yes," said Eager.

"You knew?" said Gavin. "How did you find out? I know you've a special communication system at home, but you can't use it when you're at Mum's. Did you use the gobetween?"

All eyes were on Eager. He looked back at the faces he loved and trusted. Perhaps it would be all right to tell them about Jonquil. He and his nephew would return home tomorrow, so the danger would be over. . . .

"I'm not alone," he announced. He waited for a voice to instruct him to be silent, as it had before. He scanned the terrace in case Sphere should be hovering. Nothing.

His listeners had puzzled looks. "Well, no, you're not alone, if you mean you have friends," said Fleur.

"My nephew is with me," said Eager.

There was a silence, broken by Marcia laughing. "Nephew!" she spluttered. "A small version of you?"

"How can a robot have a nephew?" said Finbar.

Gavin said, "Allegra is your sister because she's an EGR3, like you. So is your nephew the next generation, an EGR4?"

"But why nephew?" said Ju.

Eager felt a strong vibration across his shoulders. "Shall I show them me?" said Jonquil's voice.

"Not yet," thought Eager. He said, "My nephew is different from me. He's a fault-finding robot. He can enter any machine and change its operation. He entered Mr. and Mrs. Bell's gobetween and connected me to home when Professor Ogden was there. . . ."

"You mean your nephew bypassed the gobetween network?" said Gavin.

"Yes," said Eager.

"Well, where is he?" said Finbar. He put down his plate.

"Now?" said Jonquil's voice.

"My lords and lady!" cried the nurse. She was hanging over the railings, waving furiously. She bustled over to the guests. "See where they come with merry look!"

"Let's wait for Mum and Dad," said Fleur.

Gavin leant toward Eager. "So this sudden ability of yours to pick up signals . . ."

"Isn't true," said Eager. "It's Jonquil who enters machines to read information. He did it at Mr. Bell's building site, and he found out about Sam."

"Jonquil—what a beautiful name," said Marcia. "It's a daffodil with rushlike leaves. Why do you call him that?"

"Now?" asked Jonquil.

"Soon," said Eager.

CHAPTER 53

The nurse came onto the terrace in a flurry of curtsying. "My lord and lady Bell, and my lord Professor Ogden."

"Good gracious!" said Professor Ogden, catching sight of Finbar. "What a pleasure to see you again!" They shook hands. The professor's grip was firm without crushing. "We met on the Sorbjet," he explained to his friends.

"I was hoping I might meet you again one day," said Finbar.

Marcia said, "If you confided more in your mother, she could have arranged it." To Finbar's surprise, she kissed the professor on the cheek. "To think we were traveling together and I didn't know it."

Professor Ogden went to greet Eager. "We meet sooner than expected," he said, a twinkle in his eye. "Well done. I've been hearing of your bravery."

The top layer of Eager's back peeled away. Marcia let out a shriek. The nurse crossed herself. The metal-colored sheet became a golden star, pulsating in the air.

"I could have waited all day," said Jonquil indignantly.

"And here's Jonquil," said Eager.

Exclamations echoed over the terrace.

The star landed on the table and balanced on the rims of the coffee cups.

"What is it?" asked Mr. Bell.

"Eager's nephew. Eager was about to explain," said Gavin.

"It's beautiful," said Mrs. Bell.

"Like a Christmas bauble," said Marcia.

"That's a robot?" said Finbar, and stood up to get closer.

Jonquil played to his audience. He became a ball and rolled under the table. He hopped out as a sheet, swaying like a sail in the wind. He would have jumped into a flowerpot but noticed the soil and thought better of it. He bounced onto a tray that was lying on the ground and disappeared.

"He's a chameleon!" cried Ju.

"Did you say comedian?" said Finbar. He laughed. "So that's who you were looking for, Eager? At the play, and Mr. and Mrs. Bell's house?"

"Hello, Jonquil," said Marcia, bending down to the tray.

Jonquil unfurled into a straw-colored ball and rolled toward her. "Now I can see why you're Jonquil. You're the color of reeds, and sometimes you're golden, like the flower. And your fibers are like rushes," she murmured. She looked up. "Can he speak?"

"You won't hear him, he's too quiet for humans," said Professor Ogden.

Eager said, "I can hear him. His mother, Allegra, can too."

"He communicates sound by vibrating his fibers," said the professor. "He also sends messages to the other robots . . . telepathically, one might say."

"How does he hear, and see?" said Gavin.

"By sonar and radar. He sees you, for example, by sending out sonar waves and reading the echoes, as a bat does. His most extraordinary ability is to enter the circuitry of any machine to correct faults. That's what he was designed to do."

"Eager was telling us," said Fleur. "How does he do it?"

"He sends a part of himself into the machine to read its electromagnetic patterns. He can change the patterns accordingly. At the same time, he can 'watch' whatever is on the screen."

Mrs. Bell mused, "He wouldn't be a fan of *Stars in Space,* by any chance? It might explain why Eager was asking me about the show."

Jonquil jumped into the air and shook himself.

"I can't tell if that's a yes or a no," said Mrs. Bell in amusement.

"He says 'not any longer,' " said Eager.

"How can he be Eager's nephew, Professor?" said Gavin.

Professor Ogden sat down and accepted a cup of coffee from Fleur. "I'll have to start at the beginning, I'm afraid." He tilted his head as music filled the air. "Flamenco?" he said. A piano started to play, pounding out ballet tunes. "How fortuitous," continued the professor. "We won't be overheard."

He sipped his coffee, and everyone sat down to listen.

The professor put down his cup. "As you well know, there's a law against building robots like Eager. I refused to agree to it. LifeCorp had me resign, even though I gave them a solemn undertaking not to continue my research into self-aware robots. I was happy to go, mind you. They would have had me building animats for the rest of my career."

"Have you broken your word since then?" said Mrs. Bell disbelievingly.

"No," said the professor. "I've kept to the letter of the law. As to the *spirit* of it . . ." He fixed his attention on the nearest tub of flowers. A smile played on his lips. "There is nothing in the law that bans *robots* from making self-conscious robots."

His listeners needed time to take in this information.

"If I understand correctly," said Mr. Bell, "you're saying Eager and his sister have continued your work?"

Eager said hastily, "Allegra is more of a scientist than I am."

"Indeed," said the professor. "And over the years, Allegra has built a number of robots to do different tasks. Not all of them have exhibited self-awareness. When I say 'built,' it's often a case of combining elements from existing robots. That's where reproduction comes into it. Two robots combine parts of themselves to create a hybrid. . . ."

Mr. Bell said, "Is the resulting robot a cross between its parents, like human children?"

"Not necessarily in its physical structure," said Professor Ogden. "But in its memes, yes."

"Memes?" said Fleur.

"Memes are bits of information, cultural practices, habits

279

and so forth that a society passes on to its members. Rather as people pass on their genes, these robots are passing on their memes—their knowledge and experience."

"So that's how you have a nephew, Eager?" said Gavin.

Mrs. Bell twisted in her chair. "And where is he?"

CHAPTER 54

Finbar left everyone talking on the terrace and went downstairs in the lift. His mother had given him the code to open the hired car, and he quickly pulled out what he needed. The golden star hopped from his shoulder onto the roof of the car. Finbar assumed that Jonquil was watching him, though there was no way of telling.

"Like I said, Jonquil, I need your help to speak to someone on the gobetween."

The points of the star contracted and expanded.

"Thank you," said Finbar. As he headed back to the dance school, something caught his eye above. His mother and several of the Bells were waving to him from the roof. "Looks as if they've noticed you're missing," he said to Jonquil, who was now perched on his shoulder. He hurried into the lift.

"I've asked Jonquil to help me with something," Finbar said as he stepped onto the terrace.

His mother came forward. "What are you doing with that?"

she asked, nodding at the slim white box in his arms. "It was in your hotel room and I packed it in the car."

Finbar clutched the box to his chest. Ju spotted the gold lettering on the box and guessed what was inside. Quickly she said, "Aren't we going to hear about what happened at ISA? Eager couldn't tell us on the train because there were other people in the compartment. I'm dying to know."

"Of course," said her grandmother. "Let's sit down again."

From the corner of her eye, Ju caught Finbar's grateful look as he slipped through the French windows into the living area. He put the box on the floor and went back to join the others. Jonquil stayed on his shoulder.

The nurse brought fresh coffee and juice and everyone sat down to breakfast at last. As the humans ate, Eager recounted his time at the International Space Authority. The professor listened without comment, though he smiled from time to time.

"Maoz!" he said with a chuckle when Eager had finished. "A clever touch by Molly—or Major Campbell, as I should call her."

Gavin cleared his throat. "She's been demoted," he said.

"A shame," said Professor Ogden. "She's obviously talented. Still, it may do her good to be away from the general's influence."

"Yes," said Gavin quietly.

"What's so clever about Maoz?" said Marcia.

"The first serious attempt to pick up a radio signal from a

civilization in space was called Project Ozma," said the professor. "In the mid-twentieth century."

Finbar groaned. "Oz-ma—Ma-oz," he said. "But wouldn't everyone have spotted it?"

"Perhaps Molly thought it didn't matter at this stage," said Professor Ogden. "I expect the general was amused."

"Do you know him?" asked Gavin.

The professor shook his head. "I've heard of him. He's known for his unusual views."

"Sounds a bit barmy," said Mr. Bell.

"I wouldn't say that. He's a thoughtful man. I agree with him on many things. But while it's appealing to think a new leader might come and solve the world's problems, I don't believe it's the answer. . . ."

The professor turned his attention to the sweet peas climbing up the railings. "When we lost faith in political leaders, we looked to science for the answers. My old company, LifeCorp, became more powerful than governments. But when their technology let people down, we lost faith in science too. So, in a sense, we are rudderless, as the general suggests."

"Who needs leaders?" said Marcia, tossing her hair over her shoulder. "We should trust our inner compass. I followed mine and became an artist instead of a technocrat. When our inner guide tells us that something is wrong, we need to stand up and say so."

"That's why Mum is so good at complaining," thought

Finbar. "Her inner guide is egging her on." But at heart he knew that she was talking about something far deeper. He gave her a hug on his way back into the house. She looked startled, then smiled.

"Do you think the general will . . . do anything?" said Mrs. Bell.

"You mean will he pursue Eager?" said Professor Ogden. He looked across at the robot. "Rest assured, Eager, it will do him more harm than good. He won't want his superiors to hear about his plot to manage the world. From what you say, very few people knew you were at ISA, so the matter will soon blow over."

"It's an interesting thought, though," mused Marcia. "Eager as an extraterrestrial, come to teach us how to be civilized."

"I think he has plenty to teach us as it is," said Mrs. Bell. She beamed at Eager. "Why should you pretend to be an alien?"

"What about the signals?" said Ju. "Do you think extra-terrestrials are really trying to contact us?"

The professor raised an eyebrow. "Who knows? People in high places are taking the signals seriously. But as Chloe just said . . ." He winked at Mrs. Bell. "There are wise beings far closer to home. Eh, Eager?"

Eager was busy staring at a flowerpot and seemed not to have heard.

CHAPTER 35

Finbar went into the living area with Jonquil. "I want to visit the Jackson Gallery in Amsterdam," he told the robot.

Instantly, the gobetween screen showed the gallery where Marcia's paintings were hung. The view was of the far wall.

"He's here!" exclaimed Finbar. A boy in yellow and green trousers stood with his back turned, looking at the picture of Finbar. "He can't see me, unless you can turn on the gobey screens at the gallery, Jonquil."

A golden fiber seemed to detach itself from Jonquil and disappear. It happened so quickly that Finbar thought he must be mistaken. Jonquil began to jump up and down.

"Hello," Finbar said.

The boy in the gallery swung round. His mouth dropped open. "You!" he said. "How come I can see you? People are visiting the gallery—the gobey should be shut off." His eyes darted from side to side.

"You aren't the only hacker," said Finbar grimly. He and the boy faced each other, though they were worlds apart. Finbar bent down and picked up the white box. "This is for you," he said. "The turquoise suit."

The boy made an effort to speak. "But . . . you . . ."

"It's yours. You ordered it, and it was made for you," said Finbar. "By the way, I don't mind you saying you're me. I did at first, but it doesn't bother me anymore. I hate that kind of thing anyway—the parties and the fuss. Enjoy it, if that's what you want."

There was terror in the boy's eyes. Finbar thought—"I might as well have threatened him."

"No strings," said Finbar. "Though I should warn you—Mum's bringing me to Amsterdam later in the month." He smiled. "I'll try to keep a low profile."

The boy managed to utter a word. "Why?"

"Why not? This is the life you want. You can't harm me." Finbar paused. "I said there are no strings, and I mean it. Still, I'd like you to tell me what happened on the Sorbjet." He fought to keep his voice light. "How did you take over my jinn? Why did you do it? Were you alone?"

The boy waggled his chin as if to flex his jaw muscles. He said, in the flat tones that Finbar remembered, "I was with my dad and his boss. We were in standard class, and the boss was upstairs. He always travels first-class."

"Boss?" said Finbar. "What does your dad do?"

"You just said it—hacker."

"Thief!"

The boy fell silent for a moment. "Things had got hot at home, so we were heading to Europe."

"And you saw your chance to steal yourself a new wardrobe for the trip," said Finbar without bitterness.

"No." The boy sounded emphatic. "I went to the viewing platform. . . ."

"You did?" cried Finbar. "I thought you never got there."

"That's all I was going to do," said the boy. "Then halfway down the stairs I saw your mum. She was floating there in that blue dress, and her hair was like this—" He held his hands some way from his head. "It was streaming around her, and her face was shining with happiness. I thought . . ."

"What did you think?" said Finbar.

"She was so pretty. And there was something about her . . . I'd never seen anyone like her before. People pretend to have it, but I'd never seen the real thing. I thought, if she has it, you must too."

"I hope you found it, whatever it is," said Finbar wryly.

The boy shrugged. "The food's been good."

"So you decided to copy my jinn?"

"I only wanted a bit of you," said the boy. He shifted his feet. "I wasn't going to—"

Finbar held up a hand to silence him. "Just tell me how you did it."

The boy raised an eyebrow. "Took it to the boss. He downloaded it onto another jinn in seconds. He's the best," he added proudly. "You didn't notice me. I saw you sitting at the back of the cabin, looking out the window." He paused. "Aren't you going to do anything at all?"

"No," said Finbar. "I only wanted to know what happened. And your name."

The boy stared at him.

"You stole my identity," said Finbar, reproachful for the first time. "The least you can do is tell me yours."

"Elliot Dean."

"Hello, Elliot Dean. And goodbye." Finbar hoped that Jonquil would understand that he wanted to end the encounter. "Enjoy the rest of your stay," he added. "I'll post the suit to Finbar Khan at the gallery!"

Finbar must have already faded from view, for the boy seemed to be caught unaware. He heard a cry of "Finbar!" and Elliot Dean disappeared.

"Thank you, Jonquil," said Finbar. "Are you out of the gobey safely?"

The ball bounced into the air. Finbar glanced at the blank screen. Though he was relieved that the talk was over, his satisfaction felt hollow. He had wanted to know the truth and Elliott had told him. But was it the truth? Or was it some romantic story that the boy thought he would want to hear? All that stuff about his mum's hair streaming around her . . . Could he even believe Elliott's name?

"I don't know, Jonquil," he said. "I just don't know."

CHAPTER 56

"Let's celebrate," said **Mr. Bell** on the terrace. "Sam is safe, and we must toast Eager's exploits." He stood up. "We brought champagne and sparkling juice with us. I'll tell the nurse to fetch them from the fridge."

"Cold chest," said Ju. "That's what she calls it."

Marcia walked over to Gavin, who was leaning on the railings, gazing out. She stood beside him, sharing the view. The air was full of the scent of honeysuckle. Two girls came out of the dance school, giggling, and ran down the cul-de-sac. The flamenco music gave way to waltzes.

Marcia said in a low voice, "I'm sorry about what happened. Do you think you and Molly . . . ?"

"No," said Gavin firmly. "She said we don't see eye to eye. Now I've heard what the general said, I understand what she meant. We don't agree."

Nothing more was said for a while. Gavin broke the silence.

"Why didn't she tell me that she knew who Eager was, and

that Mr. Lobsang was her grandfather? Was she plotting something from the start?"

"Molly isn't bad," said Marcia. "She's idealistic. She came under the sway of a powerful person."

Gavin shook his head. "I thought she saw Eager as I do. But she and the general would have turned him into a puppet."

Marcia leant back against the railings. "If people don't fear him, they want to exploit him, it seems." She looked sideways at Gavin. "My belief is, people aren't really afraid of conscious robots; they're scared of themselves. The more you look into yourself, the darker the corners you find. That's what people are afraid of. They don't like to think they have a bad side, so they blame it all on robots."

Gavin gave a quick smile. "I think you're right. I suppose as an artist you're used to exploring your darker feelings. Like jealousy and greed."

"I try to understand them. It doesn't mean I act on them. Well, I try not to act on them." She smiled. After a pause, she said, "I've come to say goodbye. We're leaving today to visit Finbar's grandparents."

"Will you be coming back?"

"In a week or so." She held up a hand to wave. "Here's Finbar," she said. Her son came onto the terrace. He was no longer carrying the white box.

Gavin turned too. "How about a liveball game when you come back from your grandparents'?" he said to Finbar.

"I'd like that," said Finbar. "Thanks." He moved away. "You could come too, Marcia," he heard Gavin say.

Marcia gave a laugh. "Well, I suppose there's a first time for everything."

Astonished, Finbar swung round. Since when had his mother expressed an interest in liveball? Something shiny and bright sailed past him. It was a red heart. He gaped, then smiled. "So that's what you think, Jonquil," he whispered.

He watched his mother and Gavin for a moment, noticing how engrossed they were in their conversation. "Well, fancy a robot knowing more about these things than me," he said. "Must be all those soap operas you watch."

The red heart bent double, as if taking a bow.

CHAPTER 57

It started to get hot on the terrace. The champagne had been drunk. Marcia said that she and Finbar should start their journey to her parents', and the party began to break up.

Professor Ogden drew Eager to one side. "Jonquil's excursion to the Bell family was a great surprise to me, but it's turned out well," he said.

"Yes," agreed Eager. "There's something else Jonquil did. We haven't told anyone yet. He sent an order from the general to have Sam sent home at once."

"From the general?" The professor sounded stern.

"He pretended it was from the general." Eager began to wonder whether they had done the right thing.

"There's often a good reason to debrief people," said Professor Ogden. "But in this case, I suspect ISA would have kept Sam longer than necessary." He winked. "Let's not mention it to anyone. It'll be a wonderful surprise. And who knows, perhaps one day I can offer Sam a job that suits him better. He's a supporter of self-aware robots."

"But robots like me are banned," said Eager.

"For the moment."

What did the professor mean? His tone had been light, almost teasing.

Professor Ogden lowered his voice. "I can't say yet whether my travels have been successful. But I believe they will bear fruit. Give it time, Eager, and you could be officially back in the world."

"Time?" said Eager. He was an old robot, compared with Jonquil.

"You have a long way to go yet," said the professor.

Eager thought about what he had just heard. Was Professor Ogden really saying that one day he could come out of hiding?

"Professor Ogden!" Gavin walked over to them. "You haven't explained where you've been all this time. I can guess—traveling the world, trying to end the Ban?"

"I was just telling Eager that I don't know the outcome. But yes, I've been trying to persuade governments . . . I've told them that self-aware robots will want to help us. I hardly need to tell you about Eager, but you've just learnt a little of what Jonquil can do. Imagine if we had a world of robots like him, checking our machines, keeping us safe! Robots that think and feel like humans can help us because they know what's important to us. That's something an animat will never understand."

Gavin nodded. "But some countries are afraid their enemies will use self-aware robots as weapons," he said.

"It suits governments to exaggerate the danger," said the professor. "But it's true, there is always the possibility that technology will be misused. Look at medicine. We can alter people's genes before they're born. But do we really want to create a race of superhumans? We have decided no. So we have safeguards to prevent it. We should do the same with conscious robots."

He appeared tired suddenly, like a man who has carried a heavy load for too long. A flash of gold on the railings caught his eye. Jonquil was performing starbursts for Ju and Finbar.

The professor began to look more cheerful.

"Will you tell me something else?" said Gavin. "Was Allegra trying to re-create Sphere when she made Jonquil?"

"Nothing so ambitious," said the professor. "As you know, Sphere was the unexpected result of an experiment. I still don't fully understand what it is, or how it came into being."

He chuckled. "However, you are not that far from the mark. Allegra combined her memes with one of the machines that we used to build Sphere. So yes, there is some connection."

The professor returned his gaze to the railings.

"Sphere is very wise," said Eager. "It guided me when I first lived in the human world. I don't know how Jonquil has survived without Sphere."

Eager wondered why Gavin and Professor Ogden had begun to laugh. Jonquil heard the laughter and pirouetted along the railing toward them.

"What's the joke, Uncle Eager?" he said.

"I think I am," said Eager.

Eager's Nephew is the second novel by **Helen Fox**. She lives in London with her son and her husband, who is a scientist. She graduated from Oxford University with a degree in history and modern languages. Before she became a writer she worked as a primary school teacher and trained and worked as an actress.